C000029095

BROKEN: A DARK VAMPIRE ROMANCE

VAMPIRE GUARDIANS BOOK 1

ZARA NOVAK

1

RACHEL

I ran down hallways, my feet pounding on marble, the figures of oil giants staring down at me from their gilded frames. Looking back over my shoulder I saw him walk slowly around the corner, a silhouette against the dark museum interior.

In that darkness I saw two red points shining in his eyes.

Bright eyes.

Red eyes.

Eyes that weren't human.

Eyes that were looking right at me.

The corridor came to an abrupt end and I took a sharp left, banking for the *Courts of Ancient Egypt* exhibition. I could cut through here and get out the building through the southern fire escape. I could still escape while I had a chance.

But then he was in front of me, somehow appearing right before me as a blur on my vision. The blur halted about ten feet ahead, forcing me to skid to a stop.

His red eyes smirked at my terror. He hadn't even taken his hands out of his pockets. He wore a black leather jacket, a white cotton t-shirt, and denim jeans. His black hair was tussled and perfectly sculpted.

He looked like a model from a magazine, but his looks couldn't disarm me. This man was going to kill me.

I just wish I understood why.

"Why are you running from this?" he asked. His voice poured from his lips like caramel. "I can taste your desire. You *need* this."

"No," I said, shaking my head. I didn't know who this mysterious man was, or even why I was running from him, but I had the feeling I had been here before. I noticed that fear wasn't the only emotion I was feeling. An undercurrent of raw arousal beat through my chest, pebbling my nipples and making my pussy slick.

I did want this man... this *thing*. I'd never wanted anything so much in my life.

"Stay away," I said to him. "I'm warning you."

In another flash he slid through the air, coming at me like a cloud of impossibly fast shadow. The next thing I know I'm on the floor and he's over me, mere inches separating our bodies as his bright red eyes burned into mine.

He opened his mouth and I saw long fangs where normal human teeth should be.

"That's right," he said through a dark grin. "You run. But you don't know why. All you need to know is this: Your body is mine. Your soul is mine. That tight little pussy belongs to me, and the sooner I claim you the better. You're a rare one, Rachel Stone, and I will have you."

He drew my name out on his lips, taking his time with the syllables as if they were precious gems. Though I couldn't ignore the absolute lust I felt towards this man I wouldn't let myself fall prey to him.

With a sharp thrust I sent my knee between his legs and he rolled off my body. I was up on my feet a second later, running straight for the fire escape door which was only seconds away.

Then something hit me from the side. I flew sideways through the air and hit the wall hard, cushioned by the arms of the very thing that had caught me. My pursuer had one hand around my throat and another between my legs, holding me up against the wall and lifting me off the ground.

"Oh, so you're a naughty girl?" he teased through a dark laugh. I wanted to strike at the bastard and hurt him, but the only thing I could focus on was the feeling of his hand pressing against my damp crotch.

"Let me... go!" I managed, my words struggling against the strength of his hand.

"Only when you've learned your lesson," he said. "Never disobey. You've earned a punishment, little one. Time to turn that sweet little ass red."

"What? Hey!"

With his hand still around my throat he used the other to tear off my clothes. My smart trousers and jacket ripped away easily, leaving me in my soaked panties and shirt blouse. Then he dropped down to one knee and bent me over it. Before I could say a word, his hand sliced through the air and spanked me hard.

"Fuck!" I yelled, the sound echoing across the spacious exhibition room. He lifted his hand and spanked me again straight away, his palm brandishing my soft skin with pain and punishment.

"That's right, Miss Stone," he laughed. "Scream for your master. Tell me how much you like it."

I would tell him to go *fuck himself,* and that was my intention until his hand came down again, stealing the words from my mouth and replacing them with more cries of pain. Amid the pain however was an undeniable pleasure. Each time his hand struck my body my pussy clenched tight and I longed for something greater than this.

My body actually wanted him. *I* actually wanted him.

Fuck.

In a moment of good fortune, I managed to snap my foot up and connect my heel with the side of his perfectly chiseled face. I was up and running again, almost at the door when he caught me once more. This time we were back on the floor. My knees were on top of his shoulders and he perched between my legs like a jaguar waiting for the kill.

We were naked now, somehow. He towered over me as a cage of terror, strength, and perfect muscle. In all the confusion I couldn't take my eyes away from those red pearls, and I couldn't stop thinking about how much I wanted him. Glancing down I saw the long and dark shadow between his legs. It hovered only inches away from my slick opening.

"If there's one thing you need to learn Miss Stone, it's that you can't run from destiny."

He thrust forward, his huge cock penetrating me in one slick move. I cried out, my nails clawing at the floor, my back arching up toward the ceiling.

I wanted him. I wanted this. He was irresistible.

"You're mine," he growled. "Don't you forget it."

"Rachel? Rachel? Hello? Please don't tell me you're actually daydreaming right now."

"Huh?"

I snapped back to reality at the sound of Barry's voice. My awareness immediately came to the room and I saw my overweight colleague staring back at me, his hefty physique bulging out of his ill-fitting suit and creased shirt.

"Did you say something?" I asked, tucking a lock of my long dark hair behind my ear.

"Yeah. Can you get your head out of the clouds for one second and pay attention? This is only the most important night of our careers."

"You're right. I'm sorry. Where's Doctor Turner? How long until everyone gets here?"

"The old man is taking a leak. You know what he's like. As for Harkin and the rest of his men, they should have been here an hour ago. God knows what they're playing at. What are you daydreaming about anyway? Fame and fortune? If your prediction pays off this could be massive for us, for you."

I wouldn't dare repeat my daydreams out loud, especially not to someone like Barry, who had finally given up on asking me out to dinner after five straight months of me rejecting him. I think he'd finally got the idea that I wasn't interested, but if I started spouting off over-the-top sexual fantasies, he might think I'm trying to start something.

The truth was that I wasn't a natural daydreamer. I had always been incredibly focused; I had been like that since I was a young girl. I liked to think my sharp focus was an attribute to my current success. As a history and archaeology major, I had finished Summa cum laude and been awarded a research position on Doctor Turner's team at the University of New York.

Part of me considered it luck, but I had worked hard and earned my way into the most sought-after graduate position in America, and things had only gone up from there.

It was close to midnight and very much after hours at the Museum of Natural History. We were here to break open the *Shén Tiàoma* a thousand-year-old stone casket that was thought to contain the remains of a long-deceased Chinese lord.

I suspected different, however.

After months of research I believed I had found evidence suggesting a priceless artifact was hidden inside the sarcophagus. With Doctor Turner's influence and a lot of persuasion the museum had finally agreed to open up the tomb.

If my suspicions were right, we would find the Halo Amulet inside, an ancient artifact that had been lost for hundreds of years. The entire archaeology community was waiting on the edges of their seats to see if Doctor Rachel Stone was right.

I had become something of a celebrity within the field unfortunately. I was well-known as an up and comer in the field, a 'plucky young woman with a mind as great as her figure', as the antiquated *Archaeology Digest* had put it.

I didn't care for the attention at all. Half of the community had put me on this strange pedestal and the other half thought I was an irritating young woman that needed to go away. My notoriety at least had helped sway the museum into opening the sarcophagus tonight, so that was one thing at least.

But tonight, my focus wasn't with me. It wasn't with me at all. In truth I hadn't been able to think straight for the last week, ever since the details of the meeting had been put into place. During this last week I had felt as though someone was following me, watching my every move, and I had been haunted by endless daydreams that were both disturbing, confusing, and... overly erotic.

"Rachel? Hello? God. You've gone again. Where the hell is your head?"

"I'm fine," I snapped at Barry. "When are we getting started? Where the bloody hell is everyone?"

Doctor Turner returned then, as if on cue. The old man walked into the large atrium and clapped his hands together. With his tweed suit and untamed white hair, he looked every part the mad old professor. "Enough chit-chat! Where's Gable?"

"Right here Doctor Turner," a voice echoed from the other side of the room. It came from a tall and statuesque blonde in her fifties. Juniper Gable was the head curator for the museum and the only reason this meet was happening in the first place. "Harkin and his family have just arrived now. Security are escorting them. Apparently, there was a hold up at the airport."

"Hold up?" Barry scoffed. "What's the hold up? They're billionaires. They fly private wherever they want."

"Watch your damn tone, Doctor Cook," Doctor Turner said to Barry. "Without Harkin's approval this excavation wouldn't be happening at all. The sarcophagus belongs to his family, and we're sure as hell not getting it open without their good nature."

Barry turned a shade of deep red and decided to study the marble floor. "Just saying, a little heads up would have been professional. I don't see why they wanted to be here anyway."

"It's unusual Barry, but so what?" I said. "If the family wants to be here its entirely in their prerogative. It means we get to open up the vault, so what's the problem?"

"Problem?" a sharp voice said, echoing down the hall to our left. We turned and saw Harkin walking with an entourage of fifteen men in suits. "I certainly hope there aren't any problems, not on a night like tonight."

"Mr. Harkin!" Doctor Turner said enthusiastically, putting on his best professional front. "It really is an honor to have you here tonight."

"Cut the crap Turner," Harkin said as his group came into the atrium. "I know you and your scientist friends couldn't give a shit about me being here. You would have had this thing open weeks ago if you had your way."

"Not at all," Turner said. "Respecting the wishes of the living is the best way to honor the dead. As historians we must—"

"Yawn," Harkin shouted. "Let's skip the theatrics, shall we?" Harkin turned his gaze on Juniper Gable. "So, you're the bitch that won't tell me where my property is."

"Hey," I said sternly. "What's with the hostility?"

Harkin simply sneered at me. "Ah yes, *Miss Rachel Stone.* The pinup that all these old scientist geeks jerk off to. No need to get your knickers in a twist, I'm just being cute. Miss Gable is very protective of her catalog, isn't that right, Miss Gable?"

Juniper's eyes darted about beneath her large thick-rimmed spectacles. "Mr. Harkin it's standard procedure to keep our catalogue safeguarded. Your family's property encompasses some of the most expensive items in our holding. Their location must be kept top secret at all times."

"You've tried to see the sarcophagus already?" I said to Harkin. This thing had lay hidden in the museum's warehouse for three decades, and all of a sudden Harkin wanted to see it. What was that about?

"You got a problem with that?" he snapped. "The sarcophagus belongs to my family, and whatever is inside belongs to my family too, you'll all do well to remember that. If it's too much trouble I'm sure we can always cancel the opening."

"No!" Doctor Turner said, laughing nervously to himself. "No, that won't be necessary. We're all very grateful you're here, Harkin." He shifted his attention to the curator, Juniper Gable. "Miss Gable, shall we get started? Where is the star of the hour?"

She managed a smile. I got the sense that she liked Harkin and his entourage just as much as I did. "Follow me. Everything is prepared and ready. We have set aside a dedicated research chamber."

A few minutes later we were in the underbelly of the museum, in the expansive basements that housed the warehouses and research facilities. Juniper led us to a large room in the center of which was a smaller glass room. Inside was the stone sarcophagus.

"Impressive display," Harkin said under his breath.

"Atmosphere control is necessary when opening ancient artifacts like this," Juniper said. "There's no telling what kind of pathogens might be lurking inside. We will all need to suit up before heading inside. There are sealed hazmat suits hanging up on the wall to your right, though—" she paused and looked at Harkin's greater entourage. "I'm afraid we don't have enough for your men. They will have to wait outside."

"You heard the woman," Harkin said as he grabbed a hazmat off the wall and suited up. Once the rest of us had dressed, Juniper used her keycard to open up the sealed room and we stepped inside. Air hissed all around us and another set of doors opened. We all circled the sarcophagus. My heart was beating in my temples.

"It's beautiful," Barry said, his voice crackling through a speaker in my suit.

"Quite remarkable," Doctor Turner said.

"It's hard to believe we're finally opening this thing," Juniper said. "Let's get the cameras rolling."

Harkin just sighed. "Christ. Let's open this crock of shit already. Is there a jack hammer about?"

Juniper laughed nervously before wheeling over a silver cart of tools. "Procedures like this are delicate. We will have to take our time opening it up so not to damage the artifact. Rachel, would you like to do the honors?"

"Certainly," I said, my heart swelling with pride. I took the stone chisel Juniper was holding out and started tapping along a crease near the top of the tomb. It would probably take about twenty minutes just to break the seal, but care was important in cases like—

"Hey!"

"While we're young, yeah?" Harkin said as he snatched the chisel from my hands. He swung the chisel through the air in a wide arc, smashing the point into the sealed crease.

"Christ!" Barry shouted. "Be careful with that thing!"

Harkin wasn't even close to being respectful, but the way he handled the chisel made me think of some trained assassin. His control of the blade looked effortless, and I couldn't fault his aim, even if he was a giant prick. In thirty seconds, he had delivered several sharp blows around the perimeter of the sarcophagus. With one last one something cracked, and I knew the lid was finally free.

"Don't send a woman to do a man's job," Harkin said as he launched the chisel onto the ground behind him.

"Now we need to take great care removing the lid," Juniper said, looking keen to take back control. "There's a hoist above—"

"Forget that, stand back!" Harkin roared. Without warning he thrust his fingers under the edge of the seal and threw the sarcophagus lid up. I watched it spin through the air in slow motion. Doctor Turner and Barry had to scramble out of the way to avoid getting crushed. I couldn't understand how Harkin had just done that. The lid had to weigh a couple hundred pounds by itself.

"No!" Juniper shouted, vocalizing our collective dread as the lid shattered in a thousand pieces on the floor.

"Oopsie," Harkin said, not sounding sorry at all. "Now for the grand reveal."

I think everyone, Harkin excluded, needed more time to mourn the precious artifact that had just been permanently destroyed, but we were all too keen to look inside. As one we all moved forward and peered over the edge of the crypt's top.

There was no body inside.

Instead there was a tiny golden amulet, right in the middle of the stone casket's base. It was the Halo Amulet, the lost artifact that I had predicted!

"My God it's actually there," Harkin said, sounding amazed for the first time since arriving at the museum.

"It's… it's amazing!" Juniper marveled. I smiled at her. She was right. Doctor Turner and Barry were cheering. I was flying through clouds. This was huge.

"And it's mine," Harkin said. He moved forward then, lurching to grab the golden amulet before he stopped all of a sudden and clutched the side of his head. "Argh!"

"Harkin?" Doctor Turner asked.

Harkin suddenly spun around and stumbled away from the sarcophagus. When he looked back, I saw his nose was bleeding. He still clutched his head, looking like he was in great pain.

"I can't—" he said. "I can't—"

I don't know what compelled me then, but I decided *I* could. I leaned into the open sarcophagus and picked up the delicate golden amulet, holding it by the chain and lifting it into the air so everyone could see it. Then something entirely unexpected happened.

The green stone at the center of the amulet started glowing.

"Oh my!" Doctor Turner shouted. "What an interesting development!"

I stared into the green stone, bewitched by its luminescent beauty. Then I heard a click on my left and saw Harkin had ripped off his hazmat suit. He was holding a pistol, and it was pointing right at me.

"All right. Show's over folks," Harkin said as he wiped the back of his hand across his bloody lip. "The amulet belongs to me. Hand it over Doctor Stone."

2

HUNTER

She should have been a case like any other, but as soon as I saw her picture, I knew that I was thoroughly fucked.

"Doctor Rachel Stone?" I asked Davian as I skimmed the page containing her details.

"A doctor of archaeology and history," Davian clarified, as if it made any difference. His voice was gravelled and worn.

Commander Davian was large and broad, all muscle, like me. His black hair was short and spiky. His everyday outfit consisted of cargo pants, a white vest and suspenders, like some juiced-up marine from an 80s action film. He smoked a cigar whenever he was stressed, which he did pretty much all the time.

"We need you to keep an eye on her. Saydra brought it to our attention yesterday morning. Rocky got the details on her late last night."

I blew air out my lips and took a sip of blood from my mug. "That's unusually fast. Why so quick?"

And why the hell was he putting me in charge of looking after a human?

Commander Davian shrugged. "You know what Saydra is like. She is the one pulling the strings around here. Apparently, this girl is important, and she's onto something. As it happens, you're the one looking after her."

I stared at the small photo of a beautiful brunette for a few seconds before shutting the file and throwing it back to Commander Davian. "She's a human."

"Yes."

"That's not my area. Why have you tasked me with babysitting a human?"

"Look," Davian said flatly. "If I had my way, I'd let you run around doing whatever the fuck you want. Swinging your dick through the city and skull fucking demons. I know what you're into."

I laughed.

Davian had a way with words. If Guardian HQ had an office swear jar it would be over-flowing with dollars from him alone.

"So why are you bringing me this shit?" I growled.

"Because Saydra asked for you specifically." Davian took another huge drag of his cigar.

I paused. That was highly unusual.

Saydra was a clairvoyant. She saw visions and relayed them to us. That was the extent of her job. Everything after that was taken care of by Davian.

"I'm not babysitting a human."

"Take it up with Saydra then," Davian said. He blew out a plume of cigar smoke and turned on his heels before leaving my office.

"Son of a bitch."

I visited Saydra rarely, and when I did it was only to get clarifying details for a job. I was a Guardian, and I worked for the *Guardians*, a top-secret organization of vampire super-soldiers that may or may not exist.

We dealt with paranormal troubles mostly, taking care of domestic security issues that fell out the remit of normal government organizations: Hunting demons, taking care of renegade vampire covens, recovering lost artifacts, assassinating dangerous paranormal figures, keeping apocalypse at bay.

We did a little bit of everything, but we let the humans take care of cats stuck in trees.

Babysitting a human though?

That was far below my fucking paygrade, and Saydra, the Guardian's soothsayer, was going to find someone else to do her shitty job.

"Hunter!" Rocky said to me as we turned into opposite ends of the hallway at the same time. He was a big son of a bitch too, we all were. Only the most elite vampires could be Guardians.

Rocky was actually the tech guy, but all staff were trained as agents too. "Did you get that intel on the doctor lady? I had to work fast, so some of it might be sloppy."

"Yeah, looks like you slipped up. I found a pretty huge typo; my name is on the case."

Rocky just laughed.

"Ah, you son of a bitch. Don't tell me you're turning it down? Saydra wanted you on this specifically."

"That's specifically the problem," I said as I walked past him.

Saydra was a weird one. I didn't really like her, and I avoided talking to her whenever I could. She was a vampire witch, completely blind, and spent most of her time swimming ass-naked in a pool of neon-blue water.

As I reached her room, I knocked on the door for courtesy, but didn't wait for an answer before I barged on in.

Her office was pretty much a pool, with a small elevated platform to the side with an open plan apartment. The room was large and dark apart from the water itself. Bright blue lights were on the pool's floor, sending reflections of the rippling water onto the dark ceiling above.

The witch was naked as the day she was born, swimming along the bottom of the pool as she did what was probably her hundredth lap of the morning.

I kept my eyes off the water, tapping my foot impatiently before she swam back and surfaced at the end closest to me.

Saydra was an odd looking one. Her appearance changed

depending on her mood, but most of the time she had all white hair and all white eyes. I'd seen a lot of crazy shit in my line of work, but she freaked me the fuck out. She freaked most people out.

That was just her way.

"Do I need to get you a strap for that pacifier?" she asked me.

"What pacifier?"

"The one you're about to spit out."

"I didn't know you had a sense of humour."

"Neither did I. I guess we both learned something today."

"Take me off this babysitting case. Give it to Hammer or Ash. They deal with human stuff."

"Hammer is in Beijing and Ash is dealing with a hell-gate in Arizona."

"Another one?"

She simply smiled.

"It's hot up there, demons like the temperature. Look, I can't tell Davian to take you off this case."

"Why?"

"Because it's *yours*, she's *yours*. I saw it in the vision."

"Tell me what this… *vision* showed you exactly," I said, gritting my teeth to control my anger.

"I can't do that. All I can tell you is that its already begun."

"There are plenty of other guardians who could do this job. This is entry level stuff."

"Then it shouldn't be a problem for a guardian of your calibre," the vampire witch countered.

"I… why am I even trying to argue with someone that can see the future?"

"Let me make a deal with you," Saydra said, dipping back below the waters momentarily before resurfacing. "Watch the target for one hour, and then I'll give the case to someone else."

"Seriously?"

She held her hand up like a scout.

"I swear on my soul. This girl needs around the clock protection and your detail needs to start straight away. Do an hour for me and I'll get Davian to sort out another agent."

I huffed. I was still irritated I even had to deal with this juvenile shit, but an hour wasn't too much. "One hour, no more, no less. When it's done, I'm gone. If someone isn't there to take over, the girl is on her own."

Saydra smiled. "Message received. Loud and clear."

Most people might wonder how vampires walk about in the day. The answer is with great difficulty. The majority of the vampire population, which isn't all that large when compared to the ordinary human population, cannot walk in sunlight without immediately bursting into flame.

Ordinary vampires cannot walk in the sunlight.

But guardians are not ordinary vampires.

We are forged.

Made.

Created in the fires of combat and science.

We enter the academy as vampires, we leave as something else.

We leave as Guardians.

It takes years to become a guardian, and only the most advanced candidates are considered for the process in the first place. Most die or lose their minds on the gruelling path. Most find their bodies aren't capable of handling the physical changes and biological stress.

I must admit there were parts of it that were tough for me, but most of the time it felt no worse than the morning after a night of heavy drinking.

Commander Davian said I was a freak of nature. A pain sponge that didn't have any foreseeable limits. When I entered the Forge, which is what the academy is formerly known as, I had some trepidations about what awaited me. There had been plenty of rumours of what the horrifying process involved, but most of them were wrong.

The real process was for worse than anyone could have anticipated.

They broke us down and built us back up again. Our minds were shaped on an anvil of martial arts, espionage and strategy. Our bones were broken, and our bodies were receptacles for hundreds of chemical cocktail injections that gave us super strength and speed.

We entered as boys and expected to leave as men, but we left as something entirely different. Monsters maybe? I don't know. My own humanity was a long way away from me now.

I could now walk in the sunlight thanks to my training, and I could do so without instantly bursting into flame. It was still damned uncomfortable, and I still had 90% of my skin covered, but hey, here I was, walking down the street with the rest of the normies.

With a trench coat, trilby and shades, I looked suspicious as fuck, but it was a small price to pay for walking in the light. Things got a little better when I stepped inside the museum and the natural light diminished.

I took off my hat and shades and moved through the crowds like a shadow over silk. Most vampires had the ability to control humans, but most of them couldn't enhance that ability like a guardian could. Like I could.

With my vampiric power surrounding me like a shield I slipped through the museum undetected. I wasn't invisible, not by any far stretch of the imagination, but anyone that looked my way would fail to notice me or look past without thinking anything of it.

It meant I could access restricted areas with little trouble, which was good, because Doctor Rachel Stone worked behind a lot of locked doors.

I reached the end of a corridor and found myself facing a locked door. A guard stood outside it. He didn't see me until I talked to him.

"Let me in slim."

"Yes, sir, Doctor Turner, sir. I didn't see you there. Sorry."

The door opened and I made my way inside.

I didn't know who 'Doctor Turner' was, though I might if I cared to read Rachel's file. I'd just projected the idea of importance into the mind of the guard, and his eyes had taken care of the rest, making it look like I was this Doctor.

When I stepped inside the room, I saw the target straight away. She was alone, sitting at a computer, reading a book she had placed on the desk.

And in that second, I understood why Saydra had assigned the girl to me. Every ounce of my training flew out the window as I saw her.

She was tall, slim, with long dark hair and gorgeous brown eyes. Her lips were ruby red, her skin was the finest porcelain and...

I wanted her. Badly.

Holy fuck.

I had to turn around and steady my hand against the wall as all the blood in my body went straight to my dick. The room suddenly felt too hot.

Much too hot.

Christ. Who was this girl?

"Excuse me?" a voice said behind me. It was the most angelic sound I'd ever heard. Turning around I saw her staring at me. "Can I help you? Are you looking for someone?"

Yeah. You

I'm here to slam you against the wall, rip your clothes off and shove my cock in that tight little pussy.

Fuck.

"You can see me?" I said, sounding stupider than I ever had.

"Uh... yeah? Who are you? Do I need to call security?"

"No," I said hastily. "I mean... no. No need for that. Sorry. You just. I don't think I've ever seen a woman like you before."

Her cheeks turned pink. "Do you work here, in the museum? Are you lost?"

"I'm new. I just started on security. See?" I pulled out an old credit card, but in my mind, I projected the idea of a security pass. She stared at it for a second, her perfect brow creasing in confusion.

"That's a credit card for Liberty Bank."

"Oh, shit. Is it?" I turned it around and laughed before shoving it back into my pocket. "I must have dropped my pass down the hall. I should go find it now."

What the fuck was going on? Why didn't my mind games work on her?

I started for the door when that angelic voice stopped me again.

"Wait," she said. I turned around but avoided her eye. I didn't understand what was happening to me. I had fought demons, conquered evil, vanquished powerful foes and seen the darkest depths this world had to offer, but this woman… she unravelled me.

"What is it, miss?" I asked. I had to get out of there right now before I did something I'd regret.

"What's your name? If you're going to be working here, then I'd like to put a name to a face. I'm Doctor Rachel Stone." She held her hand out and I took it, finally looking into those perfect eyes once more.

As our hands touched it was like all sense of reality went out the window. Intense visuals filled my mind and clouded my judgement. Me on top of her, her on top of me. Two bodies naked and twining, lost in the darkness of chaotic pleasure and rasping. Her perfect breasts, her tight pussy opening around my thick cock.

I pulled my hand away as soon as we touched, gasping at the visions. She drew her arm back just as quickly and I knew she had seen the same thing. The most amazing scent filled my nostrils then and I knew she wanted me too.

"What the fuck…" she whispered to herself, wondering if I had seen the same the visions too.

"My name is Hunter," I said, saying anything to distract her from what had just happened. "Garen Hunter, but everyone calls me Hunter."

"You don't work security…" she said, saying the words quietly to herself, that perfect brow of hers furrowing over long lashes. "Do you?"

"Not in the capacity you're thinking," I said with a cryptic smile. I had to get a do-over on this. I'd fucked things up completely. The girl had seen me here and now she had my name. Maybe Saydra had given me this rookie job because she knew I was going to fuck it up like a rookie.

"You must have a strong *mind*," I continued, stealing the tempo of the conversation before she could respond. She had already managed to spot me despite my cloaking, and she hadn't fallen for my trick with the credit card. To be impervious to the mind control of a guardian, it suggested that Doctor Rachel Stone was a very unique individual.

She was human though.

I still had the upper edge.

"Mind?" she asked, her focus sticking on the word that I had used as an anchor. As soon as she repeated it, I knew I had her in my grasp.

"I'm sorry to do this Rachel," I said with much regret. "But you need to forget this encounter."

"Why?" she said, her eyes were now glassy, and she spoke as though in a daze.

"Next time we meet, you won't see me. Is that clear?"

She nodded absently. "But... touch."

I clenched my jaw and breathed out before turning to go. Touch? That's all I wanted to god damn do. My whole body was screaming at me to get back in there and claim her. Was she my mate? I didn't even have to ask myself.

No fucking doubt.

Saydra could play her fucking games. I would watch the girl. I would keep her safe.

I couldn't get close though.

I might do something I end up regretting.

The rest of the week had been pure hell. I'd gone straight back to Saydra and told her I'd take the job. The smug look on her face was the last thing I saw before I booked it out of Guardian HQ and huddled down for a week of surveillance.

Garen Hunter wasn't the type of guy to take a job like this, but I knew now why Saydra had given it to me. Doctor Rachel Stone wasn't an ordinary human, not to me anyway.

She was my mate.

If I had my way, I'd scoop her up, run for the mountains and get out of there as fast as possible. With a week alone I could claim my mate's body as much as I wanted. And I wanted to.

Badly.

But I had to stay focused. I had to make sure she stayed safe.

All I had to do was spend seven days in the shadows, staying close enough to make sure she was safe without her noticing me.

It turned out she was on the cusp of making a great discovery, and a meeting had been arranged to open some ancient Chinese coffin.

The hard thing about being a Guardian is that a lot of our jobs were handed to us by Saydra, the clairvoyant vampire witch with enigmatic visions. Details often didn't make themselves clear until danger was right at your doorstep.

A vision had warned Saydra that Rachel Stone needed to be protected, but I couldn't see for the life of me how she was in danger, until I learned who the coffin belonged to.

The Harkin family.

Leopold Harkin was heir to the Harkin fortune. They were one of the oldest, most powerful, and influential vampire families in the modern world, and they were rumoured to have their fair share of skeletons in the closet.

I'd crossed paths with Harkin before and I didn't like the bastard. His family had very old-fashioned ideas when it came to humanity, and they believed that vampires were above all humans. If they had their way humanity would be in chains, and vampires would rule the world by force.

Their ideals didn't mesh well with an organization like the Guardians, who worked hard to make sure that all the crazy paranormal shit out there didn't affect humanity.

We were chalk and cheese.

Or chalk and dog shit.

I grew even more concerned once I got a chance to snoop through

Rachel's research after hours. It appeared she and her team were looking for the Halo Amulet, an ancient artifact that had been missing for hundreds of years.

My stomach turned when I learned the truth.

The humans thought the Halo Amulet was just some pretty amulet. In reality it was a very powerful magical artifact, one that would be incredibly dangerous in the hands of a vampire like Harkin.

I also had my own personal history with the amulet.

It wasn't good.

I prayed to god that Rachel Stone was wrong, and this casket just held the mummified remains of a long-dead Chinese dude, but something in my stomach told me this was serious.

Security wise, the week passed by easily enough.

There was no sign of Harkin and I'd done a full screen of the museum from top to bottom. I couldn't detect any threats, and I couldn't find the stone sarcophagus either, believe me, I'd tried. The museum had it well hidden.

Visions of Rachel were the hardest thing. They'd come out of nowhere. I'd be chasing her down dark hallways. Pinning her against walls, throwing her against the floor. I'd fucked her in my mind a thousand times over, nearly bursting in my pants every time I thought of her tight pink pussy.

On the seventh day I had somehow made it through the week. It was the night of the meet and I had a feeling my services were about to be required. I was watching from airducts high in the ceiling as Harkin and his team of goons finally arrived in the museum.

What a prick.

The curator lady led them to the sarcophagus, and I stalked through the ventilation shafts, delicately controlling every minute muscle on my body to ensure absolute silence. You might not think it to look at me—I'm 250lbs of muscle after all—but my training and expertise meant I can move with absolute silence.

I could tiptoe over broken glass and a fucking mouse wouldn't hear me.

They headed down into the museum basement. It was a sprawling subterranean labyrinth of archives and research areas, but I had done my best to memorize the space in the week I had watched Rachel.

The journey ended in a large concrete room with an atmospheric chamber in the middle. Harkin quickly took over the opening, the fucking prick. I was perched above them, watching through the grate of the duct as Harkin threw back the top of the stone coffin. Then I saw the small amulet gleaming in the tomb, and I knew we were all fucked.

I had to stifle laughter as Harkin doubled over in pain. The bastard couldn't touch the thing for some reason. Rachel could though. It lit up when she touched it.

That was *very* interesting.

Every hair stood up on the back of my neck. Harkin was holding a gun, and he was pointing it right at her. Rachel.

My mate.

No fucking way.

It was time to make myself known.

I thrust my feet through the grate and dropped down from the ceiling, crashing through the glass chamber like an anvil through rice paper. I landed square between Rachel and Harkin, planting my legs wide as I straightened to my full height. His eyes opened wide as soon as he saw me.

"Hunter! What the fuck are you doing here?!"

"I'm about to execute your ass, get that gun out of her fucking face."

He squeezed the trigger and the gun exploded. Everyone gasped as he opened fire. The weight of the bullet hit my chest and sent me back a half-step. I looked down very slowly and ripped my shirt open. I pulled the crunched-up bullet from the surface of my armour-like skin and dropped it onto the floor.

"Big mistake Harkin. Now it's time to die."

3

RACHEL

I'm not the type of girl to scream. I never have been. But when that fucking giant of a man dropped through the glass ceiling and landed in front of me, I was squealing like a pig in butter.

It only got worse when Harkin fucking shot the man. I didn't understand how we had got here so fast. We were on the cusp of a brilliant archaeological discovery and now I was in the middle of Reservoir Dogs.

The shot screamed through the small chamber; the sheer volume of the sound hurt my ears despite my sealed suit. I think we all screamed when Harkin opened fire, but in the seconds after that the world was deafening silence.

Ringing started through my ears, and as it faded, I heard the stunned quiet of a room that had just witnessed a murder. I expected the man to drop to the ground, but instead the huge motherfucker simply dropped back a step, ripped open his shirt and then I heard something metallic clang against the floor.

Had he just... *had he just pulled a bullet out of his fucking chest?*

"Bullets?" the big guy said to Harkin, laughing to himself as he did so. "You need more than that to kill a Guardian, Harkin, come on."

"What the fuck are you doing here?" Harkin growled. The two of them no longer seemed to notice the rest of us.

"Making sure you have a bad day," the big guy replied.

Harkin looked visibly unsettled. I got the impression he was debating more shots, but then he moved his gun across and aimed at Barry.

"Oh god, oh god," Barry repeated in the corner as he went into full panic attack. "Oh god, oh god, don't kill me! I'm just a—!"

His words were cut short as Harkin sent a bullet straight into his forehead. "Shut the fuck up, fuck!" Harkin roared.

I wanted to scream again as Barry hit the floor, but I also didn't want to draw attention to myself. My whole body trembled as adrenaline spiked through me.

Doctor Turner, Juniper and I all exchanged very careful looks.

Harkin hadn't only lost his mind, he was dangerous.

The big guy surged forward then, moving so fast I couldn't believe it. What surprised me is that Harkin moved out the way just as quickly. The two of them were moving at supersonic speed.

"Kill him!" Harkin shouted to his goons outside the chamber. "Kill him! Get the girl! Get the amulet!"

Harkin ran, repeatedly firing his gun at the big guy until he was out of bullets.

The huge man sprinted around the chamber as he gave chase, somehow dodging bullets like they were flying through molasses.

Then something hit me.

Literally.

It scooped me up from the floor and I was flying.

For the next few seconds the world turned with a confusing blur of light and shadow. I had no idea what was happening until I came to a sudden stop. I was no longer in the atmospheric chamber; in fact, I was in a different part of the museum altogether. I looked around and saw the *Courts of Ancient Egypt* exhibition. I was on the third floor, and I wasn't alone.

The huge guy was there with me.

"You!" I said. He had put me down and was on his knees, his chest rising and falling rapidly. "What the fuck is going on here?! How did you do all that?!"

Looking down I noticed I wasn't even in my hazmat suit anymore.

My large accomplice didn't take any notice of me at all.

He'd pulled out some sort of futuristic looking tablet and his fingers were whirring over it. "Rocky?" he said, holding one finger to his ear. "I need a safehouse, something completely untraceable. Urgent."

"Hey, big guy!" I said. I marched up to him and kicked him with my foot. In a flash he yanked my leg and I landed on my ass.

"Valora heights? Brilliant. Peace out."

With another burst of movement, he disappeared the tablet device into his long leather jacket and then he looked at me, finally acknowledging my presence. The lights were low, but I saw him properly for the first time.

He really was a giant of a man.

Every part of his frame suggested muscle and might. He had short black hair, a square jaw and a strong face. His brow was thick and black, his cheekbones sharp and dressed in stubble. A prominent chin sat under thick lips, and a strong nose led up to blazing red eyes.

Yeah, bright red.

Like fires burning in the pit of his soul.

"It's you..." I whispered to myself. "The guy from..."

The guy from the visions I'd been having. The disturbing, over-the-top, panty-soaking visions.

"From downstairs, yeah. Sorry about that sudden entrance, Harkin left me with little choice."

"What the fuck are you?" I gasped. Whatever he was, something told me this man wasn't all human. What kind of man could move that fast and pull bullets from his chest like they were thumb tacks?

"Doctor Rachel Stone. My name is Garen Hunter, and I have been assigned as your guardian. Your life is now under threat and your survival is the highest imperative. I will now extract us to a safe location, where we will remain until I deem the threat over. These terms are not negotiable, so cooperation is strongly suggested. Any questions?"

"Yeah, you can't be serious?"

"I am, and you don't have a say in the matter. We can do this the easy way or the hard way."

"Well in that case..."

I don't know why I did it.

I think it had something to do with his tone.

I sent my foot flying up and kicked him in the chest. I don't think the blow did any real damage, but it took him by surprise and gave me a second to spring up and start running.

Who did this guy think he was exactly? I wasn't going to let some stranger abduct me and take me into hiding. I didn't know what crazy bullshit Harkin had pulled me into, but he had another thing coming if he thought—

"Hey!" I said, screaming as the giant caught up to me and pinned me to the ground. He had thrust me down face first and had my arms behind my back. The bulk of his weight was pressing against my rear. Something hard, thick, and incredibly long was digging against the thin fabric of my suit trousers.

Was I wet?

"Listen to me very carefully little lady," the giant whispered into my ear. "I'm a big guy and I've not got a lot of patience, especially when girls like you break the rules. So, here's what we're going to do, I'm going to give orders and you're going to follow them, otherwise I'll have to start dishing out punishments. Is that clear?"

"Go and fuck yourself," I hissed through my teeth. I'd never been so cavalier with anyone before, but something about this brute just got me fired up. I turned over so I was facing him and spat in his face.

That was another first for me.

He didn't look amused, but he didn't have time to retaliate. His attention suddenly shot to the corridor outside and he pulled me to my feet. Harkin's goons appeared around the corner.

"They're here!" they shouted and opened fire.

Tiny threw himself around me and started running for a large glass window at the head of the room. "Time to leave," he said as he cradled me in his arms. "It looks like we've overstayed our welcome."

With one great leap he smashed through the huge pane and we broke into the cold air of the night, falling through the darkness for a good thirty feet until his feet came down on the museum roof. I heard voices shouting through the darkness behind us, accompanied by the sound of more erratic gunfire.

"Put me down!" I screamed at the giant taking me captive, but he just laughed and sped up.

"Not a fucking chance princess."

As we sped across dark rooftops, I found myself wondering one thing over and over again.

What was this man?

The weight of my body seemed no issue to him at all, and it didn't impend his startling speed, and he had to be running at a minimum of thirty miles an hour. Then there was the way he jumped from rooftop to rooftop, clearing twenty feet expanses as though he was hopping onto a kerb.

I had been shouting for help, but with a stern look from those blazing reds I felt an invisible vine wrap around my jaw and seal it shut. He was controlling me somehow, silencing my protests. I was disturbed by the strange effect but shouting for help probably wouldn't have been that useful anyway.

It was very clear to me that ordinary people wouldn't help me escape the clutches of this captor. He wasn't all human, that much was obvious, so just what the hell was he? History and archaeology were my speciality and separating fact from fiction was a routine part of my everyday work.

Science made it easier to explain things these days, but in the past people resorted to the paranormal much more frequently. You'd be surprised how many historical accounts contained claims that were downright impossible.

But then here I was in the arms of some super-human man, so what did I know?

The dark city moved underneath us. Bright streets and veins of traffic passed under us in a blur. Tall skyscrapers crowned overhead as he moved towards the city centre. A light rain started, which soon became a heavy rain.

We were only outside in the torrential downpour for a few minutes before we reached our unknown destination.

The giant dropped down to street level and headed straight into the lobby of a very expensive looking building. It was late so there weren't many people about, but it was obviously an apartment block for the ultra-wealthy. A lone guard sat behind the desk. I hoped to god he would do something to help. I opened my mouth to scream for help, but my lips still wouldn't move.

The man sitting behind the desk didn't even look up as Tiny walked on by. It was like he couldn't even see us.

An elevator took us up to the building's top, and Tiny carried me all the way down a hallway to a door at the end. There wasn't a conventional key. He held his wrist against a keypad on the wall and then the door clicked open. Tiny barged in, kicked the door shut with the heel of his foot and practically threw me into the room.

The sheer momentum made my feet carry me a dozen paces into the dark room. I finally stopped when I hit the back of a very wide sofa. Looking back, I saw the giant standing in the entrance. He pulled off his long black jacket, hung it up and walked forward very slowly, a silhouette sliding through shadow, light twinkling in those impossibly red eyes.

With his jacket off I could properly make out his sheer size now. A tight grey t-shirt strained against the hulking torso underneath, and black combat trousers bulged around huge thighs. He was a mountain of muscle from head to toe, easily dwarfing me by a foot and a half.

The only light in the apartment came from the ambiance of the city outside. Large bay windows ran along the wall to my left. Rain hammered against the glass and droplets left strange shadows across the gloomy interior.

"Talk," he said, uttering the one word as a command. The strange force keeping my mouth shut broke and I gasped for air as words finally came back to me.

"What the fuck are you?" I said.

"You're the smart one. Why don't you tell me?" he said, advancing very slowly. I couldn't keep my eyes off him, there was something utterly hypnotic about the way he talked and moved. He looked at me like a lion eyeing a steak. Vulnerable wasn't the word.

"You're not human, whatever you are," I said. "A human couldn't do half the stuff you just did."

"So," he said, inching closer with each commanding step. "What am I then?" He smiled ever so gently, and as he did his lips pulled back to reveal long white fangs.

"No," I said, shaking my head. "Not possible. They're not real, vampires aren't—"

"But here you are," he said curtly. "Looking into the eyes of one. Did your science prepare you for this?"

"You said you were supposed to protect me," I said.

"That is correct."

"Then why do I get the feeling you are trying to intimidate me?"

"You must forgive me Doctor Stone, but the fact of the matter is that you are a very beautiful woman, and I am a very impatient... *man.*"

He ignored the question and took one final step, almost completely closing the distance between us. My breath shook on the inhale and I found his scent on the air. It was masculine, powerful, and somehow deeply comforting.

"You see as your guardian I'm not supposed to touch you in that way. I'm supposed to stay focused. Your safety is my number one priority. But..." He trailed off and lifted his hand, allowing his fingers to brush up my slender neck. The touch sent a flourish of fire through me. Every atom in my body came alive and yearned for one thing.

Him.

"But rules are hard to follow," he finished.

"Don't you dare touch me," I said, grabbing his hand and pushing it away. In a flash of movement, he had my wrist in his hand, holding it in the air as we stared at one another.

"You've seen the visions. I've seen them too. You're a bad girl. You need a man with a good touch. You need bending. Breaking. Disciplining. You want it, don't you Doctor Stone? A firm touch from my strong hand? I can see it in your eyes. I can smell it on your…" He inhaled deeply and looked down between my legs. "Person."

There was a part of me that wanted to scream 'go to hell', but it was growing rapidly smaller every second as his curious power bewitched me. All semblance of my defiance shattered as his lips came forward to claim mine.

His hands circled my hips, tugging my crotch against his as he pushed his tongue into my mouth and kissed me. I gave myself to him completely, lost in a moment of passionate madness that I couldn't climb out of. My entire body burned with the insatiable lust I now felt, my small hands squished against his chest, wanting to rip his shirt clean off and feel the naked skin underneath.

In seconds he had broken my resolve and turned it into shaking lust. When he finally broke away it was as though a spell had been lifted. I opened my eyes after a second of peaceful reflection and those bright reds were only inches from me. He stared right into my soul, lingering in the moment we had just experienced together.

Fuck I wanted him.

"How did you know about the visions?" I asked shakily. He had reduced me to a lovestruck schoolgirl with trembling knees.

"Because I saw them too. It's quite normal for a vampire and their…" he trailed off once again.

For a second his attention was elsewhere, as though he was trying to find another word to replace what he wanted to say. In that moment of distraction, I saw the handgun tucked into the holster on his waist. Without thinking I grabbed it and thrust it into his chest.

"What's this?" he said with an intrigued smile.

It was a very puzzling reaction for a man with a gun pressed against his heart.

"I'm willing to bet bullets poise a much bigger problem at point-blank range. What do you think?" My voice was shaking, as much as I tried to keep it steady. I had never even held a gun before, so this was all pretty terrifying for me.

"I think you're a very stupid little girl," he answered calmly. "And you're going to put that gun down before you get yourself hurt."

"I'm the one giving the orders now," I said. "Take your hands off my waist and step away from me. I'm not staying in this apartment with you."

He lifted his hands off my body very slowly and held them up in the air. He stepped to the side, looking as if he was complying with my instructions. In a flash of movement my escape was thwarted in seconds.

Inside of a second the gun was out my hands and disassembled on a coffee table to my right. I didn't even see him move, that's how fast he was. I simply blinked in amazement, unable to believe that any of this was real.

"When are you going to learn Doctor Stone? You're not getting away that easily. I'm your guardian, and I have to keep you safe."

"You also mentioned something about keeping your hands off me."

He smiled. "That I did. I think I failed to mention there's another rule. Every time you piss me off, I'm going to punish you for it."

I swallowed at a lump that had suddenly formed in my throat. "Punish me?"

I was getting the sense that this man, this *thing*, was a trained killer, so what did *punishment* involve exactly? Would he beat me? Torture me? Leave my mind broken and battered?

"Lose the clothes," he said very calmly. "Now."

"What?" I laughed.

"Don't make me ask again, or I'll get really angry, Doctor Stone. Lose the clothes. *Now.*"

My heart slammed in my chest, drumming savagely to the beat of both fear and arousal. I wasn't sure what was more unbelievable about this situation, the fact that I had been taken prisoner, or the fact that I was really fucking into it.

I felt compelled to follow his command, for some reason, but there

31

was something inside of me that felt like making this as difficult as possible.

"Go and fuck yourself. Let me go. No."

"Really?" he said, one brow lifting very slowly on his perfect face.

"What are you going to do?" I asked, crossing one arm over the other. "Make me?"

"I think I just might."

For half a second I wondered what that could possibly mean, but then I saw light flare in those dark red eyes. Something swept over me then, an invisible wave of heat that seemed to solidify my body from head to toe. I tried to move against the sensation, but I couldn't.

I was completely frozen.

"What is this?" I managed through my frozen lips.

"Undress for me," he commanded again. "Now."

This time the words sliced through the air like an iron whip. They cut through my skin and penetrated the very depths of my soul. My body started moving of its own accord, pulling off my suit jacket, unbuttoning my shirt and removing my trousers until my underwear was the only thing left.

I stood before him almost entirely naked, a lamb held in the thrall of a strange and hypnotic power. From the look in my captor's eyes I could tell he approved of the sight before him.

"Time to play a little game, Doctor Stone. Punishment for disobeying me. Discipline for making me angry."

He stalked off somewhere into the darkness, and he was back again a moment later, holding a long length of rope. He tied a loop around my neck—loose enough so I could still breathe—and led me across the apartment like a dog on a leash.

"You're such a pretty treasure that I wouldn't want to lose you," he said, tying the other end of the rope around a pole on the breakfast bar. He placed a firm hand on my shoulder and forced me down. "On your knees."

My breath raced with trepidation as I hit the floor. I dropped onto all fours, the rope around my neck taut against the restraint. This was shameful and humiliating, but I couldn't ignore the fact that my panties were soaked through from my wet pussy.

How was he doing this to me?

I heard his footfall disappear into the apartment before coming back again. Looking back over my shoulder I saw a leather strap in his hand. He stopped behind me and I felt his hands on my body, his large palms brushing over my smooth rear.

Without warning he wrapped his fingers around the delicate cotton panties and tore them off my body. I was completely naked now, and nothing could keep him from me.

"How many do you think you can take?" he asked.

I hadn't planned on answering. The question was obviously rhetorical, and he was just messing with me for his own amusement.

He didn't give me chance to answer anyway. As soon as he asked the question, I heard the strap slice through the air. It connected with my ass a second later, filling the dark room with a loud cracking sound.

A loud moan escaped my mouth as pain seared through me. My skin turned to fire, the heat flourishing up and down the naked flesh.

And then he spanked me again.

And again.

And again.

By the fifth strike I was howling in pain, begging for him to stop. I suspected however that my body knew something my mind did not. Amid the overwhelming current of pain there was a current of plea-sure coursing through my body, making my sex clench and tighten with each distinct hit. I was so wet that my juices were running down the inside of my thighs, and my breath was racing much in the same way as when I orgasmed.

Which made me notice the pressure building at the pit of my stomach. It then occurred to me that I was actually pretty damn close.

What the fuck?

I lost track of how many times the strap came down on my ass, but after a minute or so my howls of pain more closely resembled cries of pleasure. He finally dropped the strap to the floor, and I glanced back to see my pale rear crossed with thick red welts.

His heavy footfall slammed across the floor and he stopped behind me, crouching low so he was kneeling over my body. I saw something metallic flash in the dark and realized he had cut the rope binding me to the counter. He used the rope to pull me up off the floor and led me back across the apartment to the sofas.

With one sharp tug he threw me onto furniture. I landed on my back, looking up at the outline of the fierce beast silhouetted by the storm outside.

"What did you think of that, Doctor Stone?" he said to me. Warmth trickled through me at his words. His velveteen voice was fire in my soul. "Punishment enough? Or... pleasure?"

I was still out of breath, my chest rasping and my heart beating against my ribcage. Again, there was no time to answer. My captor pushed through the darkness and dropped down. He wrapped a hand around my ankle and pulled me toward him, making it look like I weighed nothing at all.

In a second he was over the top of me, my legs spread against his body, one of his hands around my throat. He kissed me and I melted into him completely. I wanted him now, no restraints. I needed this man to fuck me.

"What happens now?" I said, my voice breaking as the captor pulled away.

"I fuck that tight little pussy of yours," he growled. "But first..." He shifted down, moving his body down mine. "I have to taste."

Strong hands pressed against the insides of my thighs and forced my legs open. Hot breath whispered over the skin. The fiery sensation made my hips buck and my pussy clench. Then I felt his lips against my wet folds.

"F-Fuck!" I said, stammering at the sensation.

He buried himself in me, dragging his tongue up my wet groove and pursing his lips around my throbbing bud until I was shaking from head to toe. His mouth invaded every inch of my most intimate and private areas, claiming me for himself and casting me into a whirlwind of torrential pleasure.

I was panting hard, crowing pleasure on each rasping breath. Part of me wanted to subdue how much I was into this, but there really was no helping it. He had me wound around his finger.

My hands reached and clamped around his head, holding him hard as an orgasm appeared from nowhere and shook my body to the core. My stomach clenched and tensed through rapid breaths, my legs longed to squeeze around him, pull him up and draw him into my body.

He ventured further down then, dipping his tongue below the base of my pussy until it found my dark hole. He probed the tight ring of muscle and pushed the point inside, making my eyes widen and my mouth moan in pleasure.

My pussy, ass, and thighs were slick to the touch, as though bathed in oil. The man, the captor, *the vampire* that had brought me to these dizzy heights was on his knees between my legs, his own breath racing. I could see something new in those eyes now, a burning inferno that I had not yet seen in him.

"Now I claim you," he said, his voice low and rugged. "Your pussy, your ass. They both belong to me, and me only. Is that clear?"

I actually nodded along.

What?

Why did I do that?

"First you will beg," he teased.

I raised a brow. Was that so?

"And if I don't?"

He drew his hand up the inside of my thigh, making the movement slower the closer he got to my pussy. When he was finally there, he delicately slipped a finger inside my folds and curled it up until he found my spot.

"No more of this."

"Please," I said. My mind didn't even take a second to think. "Please fuck me."

He smiled darkly, still stroking my pussy with his giant finger.

"Please what?" he asked. It was incredibly hard to focus when he was fucking me like this.

"Please... sir?" I guessed. The look in his eyes told me I was correct.

"That's right."

The vampire stood and stripped his clothes off, revealing the body of statuesque muscle hiding underneath. He had to easily have a hundred pounds on me, but not a single ounce of it was fat.

I practically gawped as he tucked his thumbs into the waistband of his black boxers and slipped them down his tree trunk legs. His fat cock sprung into the air and my heart quickened at the sheer sight of it.

The thing was enormous. 'Pringle can' came to mind.

"Do I scare you?" he asked, lightning flashing silently in the window behind him. My eyes had adjusted to the darkness, but the details of his body were mostly obscured by shadow. He was merely a silhouette—a beautiful silhouette of perfect muscle—but a silhouette, nonetheless.

He turned his head slowly to face me, those luminescent red eyes blazing in his skull.

"Yes," I said. There was no point in lying.

"Good," he said. "I should. But you should know this." He moved through the air as a flash of darkness. Next thing I knew his hand was clamped over my mouth. He was on top of my body with my legs open around his powerful hips, the tip of his giant cock teasing my dripping wet pussy.

"I will never hurt you," he said. "I protect you. Forever."

The words nourished me only for a second. It's not that I didn't care for them, they were strangely comforting, but he thrust deep then, burying his giant cock right up to the hilt until I couldn't take anymore. As soon as he thrust forward, he seized my head in his hands and claimed my mouth once again, kissing me long and deep as his hips pulled back to fuck me hard.

He quickly fell into a ferocious rhythm, spearing my body with long and hard thrusts that dug so deep they forced my body up the

36

wide couch. My helpless little pussy clenched hard around him, trembling around the cock that stretched me to new limits.

I wasn't a virgin, I'd had a long-term boyfriend in college, but his libido was lower than a limbo bar and he was the epitome of a 'two-pump-chump.'

I'd never been fucked hard, certainly not like this, and the vampire captor speared me with such primal ferocity it left me wondering if anyone had ever fucked like this before. It was raw, special, animalistic and completely terrifying.

I'd never felt anything better.

He wrapped the length of rope around his hand and pulled it tight, choking me slightly as his hips continued their relentless assault. I was quickly tumbling towards a finish line, falling into the oblivion of utter carnal ecstasy.

"I'm coming—" I said rapidly, my words more noise than sense now. A chorus of possessive and primal grunts came from him in answer.

"Ask," he ordered.

"Please—" I said.

"Please what?"

"Please... sir!" I said, trying my hardest to keep the imminent explosion at bay.

With a single nod he gave permission.

My soul unravelled in his hands and I came, screaming pleasure into darkness as he fucked every last inch of me. I felt his cock swell inside me and stretch my walls further. With one final pump a ferocious blast of fire erupted across my walls and bathed me in fire. Pump after pump until his cum dripped out my pussy and ran down my ass.

In the dark silence he held himself over me. We kissed and pressed our foreheads together. The sound of his breath accompanied mine; the warmth of his naked body melded against me. He pulled out, leaving a void inside my body, one that would always be there.

"You're mine now," he said in a deadly whisper. "Never forget it."

I wasn't sure I could.

4

HUNTER

I held the amulet in my hand, ignoring the sound of my skin hissing around the burning chain. It wasn't silver, but it didn't matter with an artifact this powerful. Steam rose from my palm, my whole arm shaking as I tried to contain the strength of the amulet.

Harkin had barely been able to touch the thing.

He'd reached his hand out and pulled away instantly, clutching his head as blood ran from his nose. I definitely felt the same adverse reaction to the damned thing, but I could stomach its effects a little longer. It probably had something to do with the modifications put upon my body as a guardian.

It might even have something to do with holding the amulet once before.

It had been a long time since this dark piece of jewellery had crossed paths with me.

After a very long thirty seconds I gently set the amulet down on the coffee table and took a slow drag of my cigarette. Smoke drifted hazily across the dim light of the apartment. It was close to nine in the morning now, but it was still dark outside, and rain still battered the broad bay windows.

We had fallen into the ever dark.

I had been up for a few hours, having woken up with a beautiful naked woman next to me on the couch. Rachel was still sleeping now, but from the rhythm of her breathing I could tell she would be awake in a few minutes.

A pertaining chill had swept through the apartment during the night. The cold didn't bother me at all, but when I got up, I cranked the heat up so Rachel wouldn't get chilly. Humans were fragile in the most unusual of ways.

The world didn't know it yet, but we were in for seven days of darkness, and things were going to get damned cold in that time. I'd seen this once before and it was amazing how fast things started to freeze over.

My phone started flashing silently on the table. I grabbed it and headed into a bedroom to take the call, closing the door behind me so not to wake Rachel. There was no identifying information on the screen, but I knew it would be the Guardians.

"Davian," I said as I answered the phone. "I don't remember ordering a wakeup call."

"Very funny dipshit," Commander Davian breathed down the line. "Do you know why I'm calling you?"

"Because you missed the sound of my voice?"

"Like a bullet to the brain," my commander snapped. "I woke up this morning and noticed that the sun hadn't come over the horizon. I don't know why, but I got the funny feeling a fuck up like that had something to do with you."

"Last time I checked I don't control the sun, but that would be handy and all. You know, on account of us being vampires. What's the news saying?"

"Krakatoa," he said simply. I could have guessed as much. That was the explanation last time the ever dark came around. "The thing erupted for real, Hunter. Why didn't you tell me the girl was looking for the fucking Halo Amulet?"

"You gave me a 'run-of-the-mill babysitting case', Davian, and you told me not to come back to you until it was taken care of. So here I am, taking care of it."

"You're a fucking liability, the Halo Amulet is serious fucking business, Hunter, and you know it is. We need every cock-sucking guardian on this."

"Just the cock-sucking ones? Are you getting back into field work again?" I laughed to myself, able to imagine his fury on the other end of the line.

"Now you listen to me Hunter, you're going to tell me where you are and we're coming to pick you up. I hope to god you've got the amulet."

"Of course, I have. I also have the girl. She can hold it, Davian, isn't that interesting?"

He froze for a second. "Really? She's able to use the thing?"

I shrugged, a gesture that was often lost on phone calls. "She could hold it with no problem, and the stone even illuminated for a second. Harkin tried to touch the thing. Son of a bitch nearly had an aneurysm."

"What about you?"

"I can just about hold it, but no. I'm definitely not *worthy*."

"Don't beat yourself up, most people aren't. Give us your location and we'll come get you and the girl. Harkin is probably going to start a small war over this, so we all need to stick together."

"Didn't Rocky already give you the address for the hideout?"

"Yeah, he did, you motherfucker. We went and you're not there, so where the fuck are you?"

I grinned to myself.

I had purposely called Rocky and asked for a hideout to throw the guardians off my tail. The truth was that I had a place of my own, and even the guardians didn't know about it. The Halo amulet was a big fucking deal, and it could sway even the noblest of men. I had to keep my distance from the guardians until I knew who to trust.

"Can't you trace this call?" I said, knowing full well that he couldn't.

"I can, but something tells me you're not in Shanghai right now, because even *you* aren't that fast, so where the fuck are you?"

"I'm somewhere safe, and that's all you need to know at this moment. You know it's not safe for me to go back to HQ right now."

"Listen to me Hunter. We all know what happened last time. That isn't going to happen again. Trey was an anomaly, we're not—"

"Sorry Davian, I think I'm out of minutes."

"Hunter! I'm warning you—!"

"Speak to you soon, Davian. Don't wait up."

With the press of a button the call was done. Davian tried to call back immediately. I hit ignore and set the phone to 'do not disturb.' As I came back into the lounge, I saw Rachel sitting at the coffee table. She was holding the amulet up in the air. It spun slowly around in her grasp, the stone glowing lightly before her.

She was definitely the one.

I cleared my throat to alert her of my presence and she jumped up to her feet.

"Oh god! Oh. It's just you," she said, now clutching the amulet close to her chest. "Where have you been?"

"Just checking in with my superiors. Sleep well?"

"Really well actually," she said, though she yawned and scratched the back of her head. She was now wearing one of the dressing gowns that came with the room. Her hair was up in a messy bun. I wanted nothing more than to rip that gown off and fuck her all over again. "Um, what time is it?" she asked. "I think my watch is broken."

"It's not broken," I said. "It's just after nine. There's a reason it's still dark out."

"What?"

I grabbed the remote off the table and turned the tv on. The news was the first channel to come on, and images of the erupting volcano filled the screen.

"Jesus," Rachel said as she wandered over to the TV. "Krakatoa erupted? The last time that happened was in the 1800's. The whole world was dark for like three days."

"It was actually a week," I corrected her. "And things were fucked up for a long time after that." Ever dark only lasted a week, but it took time for the ecosystem to adjust in the aftermath. "Look, there are some... things we need to talk about. Do you want to grab some breakfast? I can shed a little more light regarding our current predicament."

"Coffee and sugar-loaded pastries are a staple requirement to start my day. I might even need to Irish that coffee after last night. It kind of hurts to sit down," she said sternly, her eyes glaring at me.

I bit my lip to stifle my laughter.

I wasn't surprised at all. Her ass would be tender for a few days at least. I'd given her quite the punishment. "What can I say, I get out of control when I'm horny. There's always more where that came from. You just have to step out of line."

She rolled her eyes, but there was definitely a trace of interest. "Don't get your hopes up. What do you want to talk about?"

"I can explain what's going on here. I think it's important you know. Are you down to talk?"

"I need coffee first, and pastries. I'm still trying to wrap my head around this whole vampire thing. I can trust you... right?"

"I guess that answer is up to you little lady. There's nothing I can say to change that."

"You're right," she said after a moment's reflection. "I'm sorry, this is all just a bit much. I tracked down the Halo Amulet, watched my colleague die, found out vampires exist, got abducted, and now the world has gone dark for a few days? It doesn't get much weirder than that."

I stared at the amulet dangling in her right hand. Little did she know, it was all down to that tiny piece of jewelry.

"Why don't you get dressed and we'll talk. There are some things you need to know about that amulet there. The weirdness has only just begun."

We both got ready and took the elevator down to the lobby.

A lot of rich folk were milling around, gossiping about the curious darkness, reading the news on their phone screens or looking at the news on monitors in the lobby.

Rachel and I stepped outside and she followed me down the street. The rain was still hammering down and dark clouds swirled overhead. It would look like regular night to most, but the dark clouds were actually from the ashfall currently circling through the stratosphere.

The *ever dark* was entirely scientific, but the actual instigator—the amulet tucked away safely in Rachel's jacket—was a powerful magical device.

We were only outside for a few minutes before ducking back inside the lobby of Four Seasons. I didn't make a habit of hanging around ultra-fancy places like this, but it just happened to be the closest diner to my hidden hideout, and it was also a business that secretly catered to vampires like myself.

Once inside the maître di escorted us to a table were we ordered some food. Humans didn't know it, but the more elite parts of society tended to be more vampire friendly. Rachel ordered a coffee and an assortment of sugar pastries.

"And you, sir?" the waiter asked.

"A Rooibos tea with an iron tablet," I said. "Is Bram working?"

"Always, sir."

"Then have him wait our table from now."

"Of course, sir," he said and left.

"Bram?" Rachel asked. "You're on first name terms with the staff?"

"Some places have dedicated staff for vampire clientele. *Bram* is just a codeword. The vampire host is always named Bram."

"You vampires sure have a great sense of humor, eh?" Rachel said sarcastically.

"I didn't come up with the code, I just follow it. You say you get cranky without coffee and sugar, want to see what a 250lb vampire looks like without his morning pint of blood?"

"You mean you *can* get grumpier?" she jibed. "I'm curious to see what that would look like."

"Don't be, I'll just take it out on your perfect little ass."

She blushed and looked away. I smiled. I knew that would shut her up.

A couple minutes later 'Bram' came over with our order on a shining dinner cart. He set a cafetière down in front of Rachel along with a tiered tray of various breakfast pastries. My 'Rooibos tea'— blood, if you hadn't already caught on—was in an old-fashioned tea pot with a matching cup and plate.

The waiter was dressed just like the rest of the staff, but he was rake-thin, deathly pale and his eyes had a slight red twinge to them. We were both vampires but at opposite ends of the spectrum physically. He gave me the slightest nod of acknowledgement.

"How about this weather?" he said to me. I very much doubted a vampire like this would know about the ever dark and the Halo Amulet, a few days of darkness was beneficial to our kind, nevertheless.

"Advantageous," I said.

"Indeed. Can I get you anything else?"

"I'll let you know," I said, slipping a hundred-dollar bill into his hand. Bram left promptly.

As soon as he left Rachel tore into her breakfast, reminding me very much of a lioness ripping apart a wildebeest after a hunt on the plains. I paused to regard her briefly before pouring some blood into a glass and drinking it down slowly.

From the first drop I felt immediately invigorated. The strength came back to my muscles and my senses sharpened. I took a huge breath of air and savored the amazing feeling.

"What's funny?" Rachel asked. I was watching her with a bemused smile on her face.

"Oh, nothing. Just… Well there's a huge vampire at this table and a tiny human woman. You'd expect *me* to be the one eating like a ferocious animal."

"I wouldn't take my sugar addiction lightly," she said before polishing off the last pastry on the tiered stand. "You'll do well to remember that."

"Oh, I definitely won't forget this any time soon."

She shrugged and took a long drink of her coffee. "I probably shouldn't binge like this. There's a good 20lbs of fat clinging to my ass and hips that I would love to kick."

"Please don't," I said. "I happen to like it a lot."

She blushed again, her fair cheeks turning a beautiful pink color. God, she was something else.

"What did you want to talk about?" she said brusquely.

I emptied my cup and set it down. "The amulet in your pocket. Do you understand what it is and what it does?"

"It's the Halo Amulet, an ancient piece of lost jewelry. Its historical value is incalculable."

"Well… that all might be true, but none of it is actually relevant."

Her brow furrowed. "What do you mean?"

"What you are holding is a very powerful magical artifact, one that most people would love to get their hands on if they could. You saw Harkin last night; he especially is keen."

"Why?" Rachel asked.

"The Halo Amulet isn't really valuable in itself," I explained. "But it serves a function. It is a compass, it leads to something extremely powerful: the secret burial place of Halo, the sun goddess."

Rachel blinked a few times. "I beg your pardon. This amulet is a compass?"

"Yes."

"And it points to the burial place of a… goddess."

"That is correct."

"I… what?"

"Just let me explain what I know, and it might make more sense."

"Okay."

"The device you held in your hands this morning has the power to change everything. The world has literally been shaped by this artifact time and time again. Do you know much about ancient mythology?"

"Well I'm a PhD in history and archaeology, so, yes, I like to think I know a little bit."

"Do you know much about the goddess Halo?" I asked.

"She is the youngest sister of Gaia, the goddess of all creation," Rachel answered.

"Very good, you do know your stuff."

"Hunter, this is elementary for me."

"Well what you might not know is that this ancient mythology is not a myth. It's real, some of it anyway."

"That just can't be possible," Rachel laughed.

"Bear with me, because it is. Some gods are better known than others, but as it happens Halo is one of the better-known ones. In fact, people used to worship the sun, they used to think *it* was god."

Rachel nodded. "Yup. To this day there are still tribes who worship the sun as the creator of all."

"Exactly. The sun goddess, Halo, was very popular, and is still well known to this day. But do you remember how she met her demise in mythology?"

"I do," Rachel said. "It was at the hand of her elder sister, Gaia, the goddess of all creation. Halo took much satisfaction in the attention and praise that people bestowed upon her. She took all the credit for Gaia's work and in turn Gaia grew scornful.

"Gaia decided to punish her sister for her vanity and condemned her soul. She split Halo's soul down the middle and locked half in the sun, and half on the earth. With the goddess split down the middle she created night and day."

"Exactly. Your knowledge is impressive."

"But what does this have to do with anything?" Rachel asked.

"This isn't a myth," I said. "It really happened. The gods are real, and half of Halo's soul really was condemned to imprisonment here on earth. The amulet you are holding is a compass that leads to her current prison."

Rachel blinked. "Suppose I believed any of this. Why would we want to find a hidden goddess?"

"When Gaia condemned her sister to imprisonment she did so with a caveat. She would give Halo the chance to unite her soul and Gaia created the Halo Amulet. Any human who managed to track down Halo is entitled to one wish. They can wish for anything in the world."

"Anything?"

"Anything," I stressed. "After that wish is spent Halo's prison moves to another secret location on the planet and the amulet is hidden elsewhere too. The next person to find the amulet has a chance to find the goddess again and be rewarded with a wish."

"How long has this been going on for?"

"No one really knows how old the gods are, but I'd wager at couple thousand years at least."

"I don't understand how you can know all this."

"I work for the Guardians, an ancient organization that helps to contain paranormal troubles. The Halo Amulet is the D.B Cooper of my world. It was last found 137 years ago. That's when Krakatoa last erupted."

"What has Krakatoa got to do with any of this?"

I shifted in my seat.

"Whenever the amulet is found the 'ever dark' begins. This is a period of seven days where the world is locked in darkness. If Halo's prison isn't found in that time the amulet automatically disappears. Both the amulet and Halo are randomly hidden once again."

"Wait, so you're telling me we're locked in this darkness now because I found the amulet?"

I nodded. "Are you starting to believe me yet?"

Rachel didn't look sure. "If this thing is as powerful as you say, then maybe you should just take it." She went to fish the amulet from her jacket, but I stopped her.

"No, don't give it to me, I'm not worthy."

"What? What is this? Wayne's World?"

"I'm not kidding, Rachel. Did you notice how Harkin couldn't touch the amulet? It has a similar effect on me. Only a select few are able to touch it, those considered worthy."

"Who had it last?" she asked.

"...No idea," I lied.

Rachel just stared at me, not knowing what to say. "These are all just fairytales."

"Just like vampires?" I asked.

"Let me recap a second," Rachel said. "You're saying if we don't find the tomb in a week then the amulet and Halo are automatically hidden somewhere once again."

"Yes."

"Well then it seems like the sensible thing to do is just hide for a week and let the amulet disappear by itself. We can avoid a whole lot of trouble that way."

"If that is what you want to do, then I will do it. I'm your guardian now, so I have to stick by your side regardless of the decision you make. I need to warn you however, there is one last part about this arrangement which means that it might be better for us to find Halo."

"What's that?"

"Gaia made the amulet so those on earth could find Halo, but she did not want the search to be easy, only the worthy should find a wish-granting goddess. This is why there is only a period of seven days to find Halo before the amulet disappears."

"And?"

"Gaia decreed that if the allotted time ran out then the finder was never worthy. If it happened too many times, then the denizens of earth had clearly fallen in their capacities and the amulet would be destroyed once and for all. She made a rule. If the amulet fails to find Halo three times, then Halo would be completely destroyed. The goddess and all parts encompassing her soul, the sun included, would forever be removed from existence."

"How... how many times has the amulet failed?"

"Turn it over and look at the back," I said. "A mark is added each time it fails."

Rachel looked around the room before pulling out the amulet. She unwrapped it from a cloth keeping it safe and placed it face down on the table. Two marks scored into the back told her the answer.

"This would be the third time?" she said as she looked up at me. Her complexion had suddenly paled.

"Yes. So… if we fail to find Halo this time. If *you* fail to find her, Rachel. Life as we know it?"

I snapped my fingers to finish the point.

"I'm starting to realize just how big this is now," she said, her voice shaking slightly.

"Yeah. It's one hell of a babysitting job," I said and took another sip of my blood.

5

RACHEL

"*C*hange of plan," I said as Hunter's damning words slowly sunk in. "I *have* to make this coffee Irish now. Where's that waiter?" I looked around the room but couldn't see any sign of him.

"Look we'll be fine," Hunter said dismissively. "Yes, there is a lot riding on us finding Halo, but that's exactly what the amulet is built to do. No other person on earth is more qualified than you right now."

I stared down at the amulet. The very same trinket had captivated and entranced me only hours before, now I didn't want to touch the thing.

I was terrified.

How could such a small object have such a large impact?

"You said your part of some paranormal crime fighting agency, right?" I said to Hunter.

He nodded. "The Guardians. Yeah, why?"

"Hunter this job is too big for me on my own. I think we need backup here, like this stuff is crazy serious. Is there a HQ? A vampire pentagon we can take refuge in?"

He shifted in his seat, bristling at the suggestion. "Guardian HQ isn't safe right now. Every guardian now knows that I have the amulet and it's keeper in my possession."

"So?" I asked. "Isn't that a good thing? We need a whole team of burly vampire psychopaths."

Hunter shook his head. "No. You don't understand the draw of the amulet. Its power is far too tempting for most. The guardians are my brothers, but even I can't trust them now we have the Halo Amulet in our possession. That little trinket has a way of warping people. Even the most honorable men will cut off their own hand to hold the power it possesses."

"But let me guess, you're different? You could very easily leave me for dead and take the amulet for yourself."

"It's different between me and you," he said cryptically.

"What? Why? How would that be different?"

"Because you mean more to me than the amulet does."

A strange silence eclipsed the table. I stared into Hunter's bright red eyes, wondering what he could have possibly meant by that. How could I mean more to him than the promise of *anything* else? We'd only just met, and I'm sure a man like him could get any woman he wanted.

"Look perhaps I should clear something up," I said. "Last night was fun and all—"

"Fun is the word you're using?"

"Okay… how about mind-blowingly fabulous?"

"A little closer to home," Hunter said.

"It was great, but I think it's best it was just a one off. I guess we're sort of working together now to return this amulet, and it's going to be difficult keeping a clear head if we're running around fucking one another at the same time."

Hunter sat up in his chair. "You mean the thought of my huge cock stretching your tight pussy is distracting for you? The idea of me slamming you up against a wall, ripping your clothes and taking your body… that would make it hard to focus?"

My throat suddenly felt very dry.

I swallowed and took a sip of water.

His words had painted very vivid images in my mind, images that I wanted to indulge greatly.

"Don't flatter yourself, I just think we need to be professional. The entire planet is potentially at stake here and we've got a limited amount of time, I think—" I paused, Hunter was staring off into the distance, not even paying attention to me. "See, this is exactly what I'm talking about. I'm trying to have a serious conversation with you and you're away with the fairies."

"When was the last time you saw the waiter. Bram?" he said without looking back at me or taking heed of my complaining at all.

"I don't know, whenever he last came to our table."

"No," Hunter said, shaking his head lightly. "That's not right. He's been across the room a few times since then, but he's not at his station now. It's been about ten minutes."

"You're keeping track of the waitstaff?" I asked. "Don't tell me you're not one of those people that finds any excuse to get out of a tip."

"I'm a guardian," Hunter said, putting extra emphasis on the latter word. "I guard, and I'm working right now, *guarding* your ass, believe it or not."

"Guarding me from some vampire waiter that weighs maybe a few more pounds than me? Are you serious right now?"

"I'm seriously thinking I made a mistake in coming here. And it's a mistake to have that thing out in public," he said referring to the amulet. "Put it away. *Now.*"

I kind of wanted to carry on pushing Hunter's buttons but the tone of his voice put the fear of god in me and I complied straight away. He definitely had a powerful aura about him, a leadership quality that could make people move mountains. He was a big fucking guy and I got the impression he was used to being in charge, so hearing his concern made me take notice.

"You are serious. You think we're in danger?"

"Until we return that amulet, we're in danger all the time. I assumed the waiter wouldn't know anything about the amulet, but if he does then this was a big fuck up. My intuition—"

I stopped him. "You're going off intuition right now?"

"Intuition is a very powerful force," Hunter said, still scanning the room. "My proverbial hackles are raised, Doctor Stone. I have the feeling something very serious is about to go down."

I thought he was being a little stupid, but the way Hunter was acting had me fucking spooked. "Should we get out of here then—" I began, but his eyes finally returned to mine, and I shut my lips straight away.

He spoke under his breath, barely moving his lips at all. "Look over your shoulder, by the door. I've found our friend. It looks like he was out getting company."

I glanced back at the entrance and saw 'Bram' standing with a dozen men in riding leathers. The group looked completely out of place in this high-end restaurant. They were bikers, better suited to a meth-riddled trailer park. Not only were they all incredibly pale, but a figure at the front—presumably the leader—was talking with Bram in hushed tones and looking our way.

"Hunter?" I said nervously as I looked back at him. "What's going on?"

"I'm guessing Bram has a cousin in a biker gang, and he definitely does know about the amulet. Are you good in stressful situations?"

"I don't know—!" I said, screaming the last word as Hunter jumped up from the table and pulled two enormous handguns out of his long black duster. He started firing at the entrance. "Get up and get behind me!" he shouted. I did so immediately.

Hunter raised his leg into the air and kicked the table over. The whole restaurant was now full of screaming and chaos. Patrons had either ducked under tables or gone running for the nearest exit. Hunter pulled me down behind the over-turned table and a smattering of gunfire returned from the other side of the room.

He put himself right next to the table, acting as an additional wall between me and any of the gunfire. Bullets peppered through the wood and I could hear them thudding into his body. He was taking direct hits to protect me. I knew he was a vampire, but how could he take so much punishment?

"What do we do now?!" I shouted over the din.

Hunter answered but his head was turned to the side like he was listening for something. "I killed about five with that initial burst, not including our friend *Bram*. I slammed that son of a bitch too. There are seven of the fuckers left, and that includes the leader." He lifted his guns and two clips slipped out of the bottom. He pulled two more from his jacket and re-loaded.

"Seven against one!" I shouted as gunfire continued around us. "We're screwed!"

Hunter just laughed. "Oh darling. Those are rookie numbers." He glanced up. "Nice chandelier, huh?"

It seemed like a strange fucking time to take in décor, but things were a little clearer once he grabbed me and sprung up to the ceiling like a jackrabbit on coke. Hunter kept one arm tight around my body while his feet somehow planted on the ceiling. With his freehand he fired at the bikers below, who were now filing deeper into the restaurant as they re-loaded their own weapons. I saw sawn-off shotguns, sub-machine guns, and even automatic rifles.

These guys weren't fucking around.

As soon as Hunter's gun clicked empty his hand moved in a blur and then he was holding a long silver blade. He slashed it across the chandelier's main cable and the fitting dropped through the air like a meteor from space. The huge chandelier crushed two more of the vampires. Both of them promptly went up in flame. I wish I had more time to appreciate how *strange* the spontaneous immolation was, but there was no time.

"Hunter!" I screamed, delirious as he sprung off in another direction, running from a new tide of gunfire. Everywhere we went the wayward whistle of bullets exploded the scenery around us. We crashed behind the bar for cover and he quickly jumped back up to his feet.

"Stay here a sec, I'll finish this."

He was gone before I could protest. To my left I saw a middle-aged woman shaking on the floor next to me. She was one of the waiters from the restaurant. "It's going to be okay!" I said to her in reassurance.

I popped my head up over the bar to see what was happening with

Hunter, but I could only see strange shadows flashing through the air. I realized it was Hunter and the other vampires fighting, all moving far too fast for my mortal eyes.

They all slowed to a more normal speed at once. Three of the bikers were left now and Hunter had somehow disarmed all of them. He was currently tangled in a three-way martial arts fight against the bikers, who didn't look as proficient in combat as he did.

For a giant motherfucker he moved with a startling grace and speed, twisting, turning, dodging and ducking as he delivered his dangerous blows. His silver blade danced through the air as a trail of death.

He plunged the point into the chest of one of the bikers. The vampire went up in a spout of flame. The fire barely died out before Hunter staked the other two. He finally came to a stop, his great chest hulking as he tried to reclaim his breath. He found me and let out a sigh.

"I think we're done," he said. But as soon as he muttered the words another group of bikers appeared in the doorway. They all had guns pointed at him. The vampire at the front of the group cautiously stepped forward.

"All right big guy, you've proved you can fight, but there's plenty more of us. Give up the trinket and no one else gets hurt."

Hunter turned toward the leader. There was no way he was finished fighting, but I had a bad feeling his luck wasn't going to stretch this far. I really wished I could help somehow. I had no idea how until a voice whispered through my mind. It was female and strangely ethereal, the words carrying a brilliant warmth that flowed through my entire body.

"Give it to them," it said. "Now."

Giving away the amulet was the last thing I wanted to do, but I realized then the warmth flowing through my body was coming from the amulet. The heat grew rapidly hotter. I pulled the amulet out and through the cloth I could see the stone glowing bright red.

"Now!" the voice shouted. "Throw it! Now!"

I was a mere spectator in my own mind. I stood up, held the cloth-wrapped amulet in my hand and hurled it towards the biker group like a grenade. I think Hunter was the only one to see me stand, but the bikers took notice of something flying towards them.

Why the hell was I acting so stupidly? I had just taken our most prized possession and thrown it right at the 'bad guys'.

"Rachel!" Hunter shouted in disbelief, wondering why I had just given away our trump card. I couldn't blame him; I was wondering the same thing myself.

The wrapped amulet hit the thick carpet like a lead weight and stopped at the feet of the lead vampire. He glanced at me then looked down at the glowing package. "Is this...?" he said, before crouching down to pick it up. "Good girl," he said to me. The amulet was glowing so brightly now it projected warm orange light through the cloth and onto his face. "Unfortunately, we'll still have to kill you bo—"

The rest of his threat went unheard as a tremendous ball of blinding light exploded through the restaurant. I had to shield my eyes from the light, hearing the screams of the vampire bikers echoing through the room as I turned away from the blast.

This explosion wasn't one of fire and force.

I was a historian, so I'd never actually witnessed an explosion—they don't happen that often in my line of work—but I knew something was off here. The blast was more like an extremely condensed burst of sunlight. For a few seconds I could see the insides of my own eyelids, before darkness came back again.

As I felt the warmth recede, I opened my eyes again and saw that the biker gang were gone, presumably burnt to a crisp. The amulet was back on the floor where I had thrown it. A surge of panic suddenly swept through me as I remembered Hunter.

"Hunter!" I shouted. I vaulted over the bar and ran to the last place I saw him standing. He was crouched down on the floor with his long black duster thrown over him like a cloak. A light curtain of smoke wafted up from his back, streaming from the various bullet holes within the leather. For a second I wondered if he was alive, then his huge figure shifted. He placed his hand on a chair and slowly stood up while letting out a very weary groan.

"Hunter," I gasped upon seeing his face. The left side of his face was unharmed, but the right side was almost charred black. "Are you… okay?" I asked, but even as I said the words, I saw his face was rapidly returning to its normal color. His ability to heal was outstanding.

"Nothing a bit of after-sun won't help," he joked. "How did you know the amulet would do that?"

"Do what? I don't even know what happened. The amulet got really hot in my pocket and there was a voice in my head telling me to throw it."

"Looks like Halo might have offered you a little guiding advice. That was an explosion of raw sunlight. It vaporized our vampire friends immediately. My tolerance for sunlight is much higher because of my Guardian modifications, but that was tough even for me."

"I'm sorry," I said. I felt sick to my stomach at the thought of hurting Hunter. "I didn't know what was happening."

"It's okay princess," he said. "Let's just add it to your list of things to be punished for. You saved our bacon anyway, there's only so many grunts I can take on at once." Sirens blared in the distance outside, Hunter looked back at the entrance. "We better get a move on before more trouble arrives. It won't be long before the police are here. Grab the amulet, quickly."

I ran over and scooped the amulet back into my jacket. The cloth surrounding the metal was still hot to the touch from the explosion of light. The restaurant was now a complete and utter wreck. Chairs and tables were overturned, shattered glass covered the floor and the intricate molded ceilings had been destroyed by gunfire.

I walked past the downed chandelier. The staff and customers had long since left. It looked like no civilians had been hurt during the firefight, which was great.

"We take the rear exit," Hunter said as he scanned the room. Something told me he had mapped out an escape route before we'd even sat down. I'd only seen a glimpse of his abilities so far, but I got the impression his guardian training was very extensive in all aspects of survival.

Without another word we left through the back. The kitchens were deserted, and I followed Hunter through a maze of service corridors. He walked with strict confidence, looking like he'd taken this route a hundred times before.

Fire doors led into an alleyway behind the building, where rain continued to sprinkle down. It was still dark outside—naturally—and I found myself thrown off by the lack of sunlight. It had to be close to midday right now, but it was dark as midnight.

"Where to now?" I asked.

"Back to the safehouse," Hunter answered. Without warning he threw me over his shoulder and vaulted straight into the air. He moved so fast I didn't even have time to scream. I wondered what was wrong with walking back the way we'd come, but the sirens outside the front of the restaurant were answer enough.

The single jump took us up ten stories, and the massive vampire landed on the rooftop of a building adjacent to the Four Seasons. Up here the world was a forest of air-conditioning units and large ventilation pipes. Every building looked the same.

Hunter broke into a sprint and a cold wind rushed over me. I was still hoisted over his shoulder with my ass in the air, looking like a cavewoman being captured by a caveman.

He does have some caveman-like qualities.

With another mammoth jump we ascended to an even higher rooftop. He set me down and sent his foot through the door of a stairwell. Inside of a minute we were back in the corridor that led to the suite.

"Talk about a lousy breakfast," he joked as he shut the door behind us. He pulled off his jacket and made his way into the apartment. I felt a strange sense of relief at being alone with him again. Danger was far behind us and we were alone together once more. Hunter headed for the bathroom, leaving me to collapse on the couch and contemplate the craziness of our brief outing.

I pulled the amulet out again, unwrapped it from the cloth and studied it. I really wish we could just wait the week out and let this thing disappear, but as things stood, we didn't have a choice. If we didn't find Halo before the end of the week then the goddess would blot out the sun permanently.

"This is too much," I whispered to myself. We'd gone out for breakfast and nearly ended up dying. Hunter didn't want to call for backup, but I couldn't help feeling we were out of our depth here. There had to be some way I could convince him. But how?

Then I heard a faint buzzing sound in the apartment. It was coming from Hunter's jacket. A phone! Of course. His superiors were probably contacting him again. I could take the call and tell them where we were!

With a quick glance toward the bathroom I got up and ran over to his jacket. The thing was huge and just from handling it I could feel its immense weight. How did he walk around in this thing? I found the phone and pulled it out. There was no ID on the screen, but I answered, nonetheless.

"Hunter, it's Commander Davian. Rumor has it some vampire prick just started a firefight in the fucking Four Seasons, of all places. Why does something tell me this has your name all over it?"

I breathed back down the line, wondering if I should have taken this call.

"Are you listening to me dumbass?! Did they shoot your fucking tongue out?! Tell me where the fuck you are, and this can all be over. You need backup!"

"This isn't Hunter," I said. "It's Doctor Rachel Stone. Who am I speaking to?"

He didn't answer straight away. "The girl. The one with the amulet."

"That's right, now tell me who you are."

"I'm Commander Davian. I'm Hunters direct supervisor and I'm here to help you. Can you tell me where you are so we can send backup? You might have realized by now that Hunter likes to fuck things up in his own special way."

"I'm starting to pick up on that," I said, laughing lightly to myself. "Look I think we need backup too, but he was hesitant to call you guys in. Can I trust you?"

"Right now, we're the only people you can trust darling. Don't hold it against Hunter, but he's got shit in his own past that makes it hard for him to trust people. He works alone now, but it wasn't always that way. His last partner fucked him over and left him for dead."

"So, one of your guardians has turned on Hunter before. What's to say that won't happen again?"

Davian huffed down the line. "Look I can't get into the details. That's for Hunter to tell you, if he wants to."

I breathed down the phone, asking myself if I could trust these people or not. From the sounds of things Hunter had every right to be suspicious of his guardian brothers, especially with the powerful draw of the amulet. I didn't know what to do.

Then I heard her voice again, whispering through my mind like a summer's breeze.

Trust him, Halo said. *We need him.*

"Doctor Stone?" Davian said.

I let out a long and regretful breath. "We're in some fancy apartment building not far from the Four Seasons. It's the tallest building on the block, I don't know the name. A suite right at the top."

Davian just laughed back down the line. "I know the place. I should have known Hunter was holed up there. Stay put and don't let Hunter know we're coming. We'll be there as fast as we can. You made the right decision Doctor Stone."

"I sure hope so." The line went dead and I put the phone back into the jacket. I turned around and saw Hunter. I gasped his name. "Hunter!"

"I only caught the last part of that conversation, but I get the distinct feeling you just betrayed me."

"The amulet told me to," I said. "*She* did. She said we couldn't do this without the guardians!"

"Did she? That's funny, because she's telling me to chain you to a bed and tan your ass until you're screaming. What do you think about that?"

"You stay the fuck away from me," I said through gritted teeth. "Every decision you have made so far has just got us into more trouble! I'm fixing this!"

Hunter laughed and stepped forward. "You're a disobedient nightmare, and you're going to learn that your actions have consequences."

The huge giant marched forward and swept me off the floor with no problem. I pounded and kicked at him, but my blows meant nothing against a man that could take bullets. In a few giant strides we had crossed the apartment and he kicked open the door to a bedroom.

He moved with a ferocious grace that was both terrifying and arousing. He hurled me onto a bed and moved as a flash in the dark.

In that moment of rapidity, I found my wrists and ankles had been shackled to the bedframe. I was on my front, my breath racing in the dark, waiting for the absurd punishment he had lined up for me. Hunter crouched down beside the bed, drawing his eyeline level with mine. His red eyes glinted with an assuming wickedness.

"Let's get started, shall we kitten?" he said. "There isn't much time before my brothers show up."

Then he was behind me. Strong hands yanked my trousers down my legs, taking my panties down too until my naked rear was exposed to the air. I felt his hand smooth delicately over my rear before he spanked me hard. I was still sore from before and I howled from his touch.

I also felt myself growing wet.

Fuck. Not again.

Hunter chuckled in the darkness. He was a fucking madman, but maybe I was the mad one, because every fiber in my body coiled with excitement.

"I'm gonna make you scream, little girl," he teased. "And then I'm going to fuck your brains out."

I had no reply. All I could do was challenge him.

"Just try it," I said, biting my lip in anticipation.

6

HUNTER

*T*he fire of rage fucking consumed me, but its heat was nothing compared to the desire I felt for my mate. I sliced my hand through the air again and spanked her hard, the sharp sound cracking through the room along with her cries of pleasure.

Yeah, pleasure. It wasn't hard to see that she was fucking into this.

Each time I brought my palm down on that sore little ass she bucked against me, grinding her naked pussy against the sheets and flooding the room with the scent of her arousal. I'd been fucking rock-solid since fucking her last night, and I couldn't wait to take her again.

The guardians would be here soon, and I knew I didn't have long before they were kicking down that door.

Getting away wasn't an option now, they'd be able to trace my scent from the apartment so I might as well stay put and teach Rachel a few lessons about discipline.

"Tell me you're sorry," I growled as my hand cracked against her rear again. She squealed in response , her entire body shaking as she succumbed to dark gratification.

I curled my finger between her silken thighs and ran the pad along her slick groove, nestling at the folds and pushing inside of her. Her pussy squeezed around my finger and she whispered a *'Fuck yes,'* pressing her face into the bedding so not to be heard.

A dark smile tugged at my lips. She wasn't going to hide this satisfaction from me.

With my finger stroking her walls I let my thumb find her other hole and probed it lightly. Rachel pushed her weight back against my hand, her body begging me to go further.

"Please—" she said, her voice trembling on her lips. I was taking my time with her, teasing her, keeping her release at bay until I heard the words I wanted to hear.

"Please what?" I asked.

"Please… let me cum," she begged.

Her desperation only made me go slower. She wasn't getting what she wanted until I heard her yield to me.

"Tell me you're sorry," I repeated, my finger moving in and out of her with a slick pulse. I was so fucking hard I could have exploded right there. Looking down at her throbbing pussy made me mad horny.

"Fuck you—" she gasped again, demonstrating that stubborn playful side of hers. She was able to hold her own when it came to it, I had to give her that.

"Not until I hear those magic words," I said, pulling my hand away from her body. I sucked her juices from my fingers and then I spanked her hard again, leaving a few seconds between each hit as I turned her creamy little ass brazen red.

I gave her ten more spanks for good measure. Each time her cries grew louder, and her physical reaction was stronger, her whole body tensing and shaking as she grew more aroused. I didn't hold back at all; I gave her the full brunt of my punishment. Enough to keep her ass sore for a day or two.

"Okay, okay!" she panted, dropping her forehead against the covers. "I'm sorry, I'm fucking sorry!"

"For?" I smoothed my palm gently over her tender skin, teasing my finger back into her folds again.

"For betraying you. I should never have gone behind your back like that."

"Who's your master?" I asked.

"Y… You are," she said.

"Who do you belong to?"

"You," she said, with less hesitance this time.

"Who owns that dirty little body of yours?"

"Y-You do," she said again.

"You're goddamn right, and if I give you orders from this point on you follow them. Clear? Or there will be repercussions."

"Yes."

"Yes, what?"

"Yes, sir," she said.

"Good girl."

I let my finger slip back inside of her and started fucking her again. With my freehand I dropped my trousers, pulled my cock out and stroked my aching shaft. I was harder than granite and wanted nothing more than to bury deep inside of her.

Only a few seconds went by after she finally succumbed to me. Then she found her reward. It came as a blinding orgasm that left her calling my name and shaking on the bed in the dark. Her pussy clenched around my finger, her entire body tensing until she finally dropped to the mattress, giving her weight back to gravity.

Heady breaths came from her spent lungs. I left her on the bed for a second to wallow in the darkness. She'd had hers and now I was going to have mine. When I came back to the bed a few moments later I was completely naked. She felt me climb onto the mattress and looked back to see my naked form. Her pupils dilated.

"Now you get the real reward," I said, moving forward until I was over her, my erection jutting into the air. I mounted her from behind, pressed my cock up against her tight opening and sank inside. Her tight lips spread around me.

Fuck. Yes. Heaven.

"Hunter…" she said, moaning my name over long and stretching syllables.

I pushed all the way inside until my cock was completely buried. Her precious little ass looked so fucking good from behind. I took her in my hands and squeezed as her tight little pussy stretched around me.

With a sharp movement I pulled my hips back and slammed forward again. Her hands strained against the restraints and reached out to grab at the bedding. I fell into a rhythm quickly and started fucking her hard.

Sweat began to drip down our bodies. I leaned in close, my chest pressed against her back as I speared her hard from behind. I wrapped my hand around her throat and pulled her up to meet me, turning her head so I could kiss her. Breath raced from her nose as my tongue dominated her mouth.

The bed bounced beneath the force of my weight. Tiny mews of pleasure hummed from Rachel's lips. My speed and force increased with each rhythmic stroke, until I was slamming into her tight pussy with a tempo that was long and deep, digging as far as I could.

Our lips broke away from one another momentarily. I kept my hand around her throat, her hot breath wicking my face as I pulled her closer to the edge.

"Yes, yes, yes—" she said on trembling whispers. I felt my cock swell inside of her as I too came close to the point of breaking.

She screamed the word again as fire exploded through her. The lust and rage swirling inside me had taken away the man and left some primal fucking animal, rutting his mate with a ferocious intensity that had no limits.

As she came, I exploded too, my cock bursting deep inside her tight pink walls, completely filling her with plumes of my molten come. She clenched around me, her pussy begging me to stay deep inside and never stop pumping.

My breath was primal and heavy, shaking in her ears like a caveman. I found her lips again and claimed them, kissing her long and deep until our rhythm finally crested into stillness.

For a small amount of time we just lay there in the darkness, my body pressed against hers, my cock still inside as my juices ran down her thighs. Sweat drenched our skin, melding our bodies together.

When we finally parted I felt something new between us, as though the already inseparable bond had deepened once again, cementing the love that I already had for her.

I untied her, wishing that I had more time to fuck every last inch of that body. Whatever tension there had been before, it was gone now. We had formed a wordless bond. I was hers; she was mine. Nothing would come between that.

That moment of peaceful silence didn't last long.

Rachel flinched when the front door flew open.

The bastards kicked it so hard it flew straight off its hinges and into the apartment. It made a real loud clatter.

"Hunter?!" she shouted, standing up and drawing the covers around herself.

"Just the guardians," I said calmly. "Backup has arrived, darling. Don't worry yourself. There's nothing we can do now. Davian probably thinks I've gone rogue."

"Come out Hunter!" a deep voice bellowed through the apartment. It was Commander Davian himself. The bedroom door flew open and I saw a team of six armed guardians all looking back at me with guns pointing in my direction. Riot armor obscured their faces completely, but I knew the one at the front, the one closest to me, was Briggs.

"Christ, you just couldn't keep your dick in your pants, could you?" Briggs said.

"Fucking do it already," I said. "You hurt the girl and I'll chop your fucking dick off."

Briggs fired the tranquilizer. The arrowed dart sank into my skin and started pumping chemicals through my body. There wasn't much that could down a guardian. This special tranquilizer had been designed to handle the impossible job.

Barely seconds went by before I felt my eyes grow heavy. The room went dark and I felt my weight slam against the bedroom floor.

Rachel had got her wish.

We were in the hands of the guardians now.

7

RACHEL

I couldn't help feeling like I had seriously fucked up somewhere down the line. As soon as Hunter's naked body hit the floor, I got a terrible feeling in my stomach that I should have listened to him.

As soon as he was down two giant figures dragged his unconscious body out the room and another stepped into the doorway. I had anticipated a knock on the door when I spoke to Hunter's superior on the phone, instead they'd sent a fucking vampire swat team.

The soldier looking at me lifted his riot visor and revealed the face of a middle-aged man. He had a solid face, like Hunter, with a square jaw, a strong brow and sharp red eyes. A sprinkle of silver stubble covered his face.

"You must be Rachel. I'm Commander Davian, Hunter's direct superior."

"Where the fuck are you taking him?" I asked. "I thought you were on our side."

"Relax Doctor Stone, we are," Davian said. He pulled a cigar from somewhere on his person and lit it before taking a long drag. "It's Hunter we're not sure about. The amulet is a very powerful device and it has a way of warping the minds of those around it."

"That's exactly why he didn't want me to call you," I said. "He didn't want you and your men to betray us over the amulet. It looks like he was right, and I was wrong. I should never have told you where we were."

"On the contrary," Davian said, blowing smoke into the room. "Hunter was exactly right. We can't be trusted around the amulet, but neither can he. Until we get a good look at him and know his mind is secure, we have to take every precaution. So far everything he has done has been off the book, which suggests he's keeping you to himself so he can steal the amulet at the last minute."

"You're dead wrong," I said, gritting my teeth. "He's a good person, he wouldn't do that."

Davian shot me a confused look. "You seem awfully attached to him, considering you barely know the guy. You know, guardians aren't supposed to sleep with their clients? He's broken a lot of fucking rules in the short time you've been around."

"And you're supposed to be his brothers in arms, right? This seems like a very strange way to say hello."

"Get up and get dressed. I'm going to wait outside and give you a minute to get ready. If you take any longer then I *will* send someone in to help you hurry the fuck up. Do you have the amulet on your person?"

"Yes, and you're not getting it."

"Good, and make sure it stays that way. It's already made its mind up and decided you're the keeper, I'm not going to act like a fucking moron and try to take it from you. My men are all under strict instructions to stay the fuck away from the thing, if anyone of them approaches you then tell me straight away. Clear?"

"Wait," I said. "You *don't* want the amulet?"

"It's only going to warp my mind and make me do something stupid. I don't really feel like killing a whole squadron of my guardians over a petty piece of fucking jewelry, so no, I don't want it."

"I don't understand then, you're not betraying us?"

"Wow, there's not much between the ears here is there? I thought you were a fucking doctor."

"I am, I'm just confused because you rocked up and hogtied the only person protecting me so far."

Davian rolled his eyes. "The equation is very simple, darling. The amulet has chosen you as its keeper. Hunter has been assigned to keep you safe. We keep Hunter safe. Once we've made sure he's not lost his fucking mind, we'll return your little lapdog and you can fuck all night long while you run the amulet back to Halo. That clear?"

"I think so. You swear a lot, you know that?"

"Shut the fuck up and get dressed," Davian said, smiling slightly around his cigar. "We leave in two fucking minutes."

The door slammed shut and I turned on the bedside light. I quickly dressed and sat down on the edge of the bed, holding my head in my hands as I tried to process everything. Were the guardians on our side or not? I had no idea who to trust.

It was possible that Hunter *had* lost his mind, but he'd directly refused the amulet from me already, just like Commander Davian had. His insubordinate streak was probably fair cause for Davian to suspect Hunter, but did they have to barge in here and shoot him like he was some escaped lion?

As I got up from the bed I wondered if this was just part and parcel of how the guardians liked to act. From the little Hunter had told me they represented the most alpha vampires in society. This organization took the toughest bastards they could find and then subjected them to grueling modifications to forge them into super-soldiers.

They were crass and abrasive. Giant pillars of arrogance, testosterone and muscle. They might be incapable of manners and civil discourse after their intense training. I guess I might feel more inclined to settle an argument with a gun too if I was pumped full of testosterone and rage.

I was barely at the door when Davian hammered his fist against the wall. It was merely to rouse me, but I could hear the plaster cracking under the weight of his hand.

"Are you fucking ready or what? Get your panties on and hurry the fuck up!"

I pulled the door open and saw Davian staring back at me, along with two more guardians. They had paid me the respect of decency at least, though I couldn't say the same for Hunter.

"Where is Hunter?" I asked.

"He ran out to buy tickets for the cocksuckers convention," Davian snapped. "Where the fuck do you think he is? Briggs and Mac have taken him up to the ship. We're going too. Move your ass."

There was no room to argue with Davian and his sailor mouth. I walked past the shattered front door and out the apartment. Two guardians were waiting for me in the corridor. They started walking and I followed, flanked by Davian and the other soldiers. The unit headed up to the roof, which was empty by all appearances.

I wondered if they were playing some stupid joke when a futuristic looking ship suddenly appeared before me. The air rippled at first, like water flowing over glass, and then the sleek black craft materialized from thin air. The thing looked like it had come straight out of a sci-fi movie.

Davian just smirked at me as he walked by. The look on my face was clearly amusing to him. "What's the matter, doll face?" he said. "Never seen an invisible ship before?"

"Sir, that's a fucking dumb question sir," one of the guardians said. "How could she see an invisible ship?"

"Shut the fuck up, Hammer," Davian said, but he laughed to himself.

"Just who are you people?" I said to Davian. Super-soldier vampires were one thing, but invisibility cloaks and futuristic fighter planes?

"We're the guardians, darling." Davian threw his cigar to the floor and crunched it under his large black boot. "Now get the fuck on board. We've got a planet to save."

"Doctor Rachel Stone, welcome to Sparta."

I took the hand of the faceless guardian as he helped me off the aircraft and I found myself standing in an underground air hanger. I'd had no chance to see the HQ from the air, but I got the distinct impression that most of the building was hidden underground anyway.

The guardian lifted his visor to reveal another strong-featured face. Long dark curls and a strong roman nose reminded me of someone.

"Name's Rocky," the guardian said as the others unloaded from the plane. I was nervously scanning for any sight of Hunter, but I couldn't see him. Davian was on the other side of the landing area, shouting orders at his men. Rocky offered his hand and I took it.

"Like the boxer?" I asked.

"Everyone gets a nickname when they enter the unit, that's mine. I'm the tech guy really, but I go into the field when I'm required."

Sizing Rocky up I estimated he had to be the biggest 'tech guy' on the planet. He was just as tall, broad and muscular as his colleagues, but I could tell he didn't have the same meathead attitude as the rest. He was a little more softly spoken and I hadn't heard a cuss yet.

"What does tech support involve for the guardians? Showing them where the space bar is on a keyboard?"

Rocky laughed. "They might look stupid, and they certainly act dumb, but I can assure you most of it is for show. You don't get into the guardians on brawn and alpha prowess alone, they want soldiers with brains too. Most of the guys here had a GPA of 4.0 back in the real world. Heck, Charge is the fucking dumbest guy in Xerxes unit, and he's got a PhD in chemistry."

"Hey, fuck you too!" a guardian said from across the landing pad. "You've got to know a thing or two about chemistry when you're blowing shit up all day."

"Xerxes unit?" I asked. "What's that?"

"That's our unit within the Guardians," Rocky explained. "Guardians work in small units, usually around six, but there's ten big fucks in Xerxes unit." He leaned in, pretending to whisper. "That's because Xerxes is the best fucking unit in the whole Guardian organization."

"Best at always fucking things up," a voice said from behind us.

Looking around I saw another huge vampire approach. He had medium length blond hair which was slicked back. He was all testosterone, just like the other guys, but I got an unsettling feeling from him. "And then Cerberus unit has to come in and clean up your shit."

"I take what I said back," Rocky said to me. "*This* is the dumbest guardian."

"Take no notice of dick lips here," the guardian said, he thrust his hand forward. "Name's Chase, I'm top dog in Cerberus. You must be the girl everyone is talking about. Let's see this amulet then."

"Back to fucking work!" Davian roared as he came barreling over. Rocky and the other guardians instantly stood up straight as their superior approached, but Chase hardly took notice.

"What the fuck are you doing here, soldier?" Davian said to Chase.

"Just making sure the most retarded unit got in okay, *sir*," Chase said.

"This area is strictly off limits to all guardians outside of Xerxes unit, and you know it. Now get your ass back to Commander Gavel and make sure I don't see you again."

"Sir, yes, *sir*," Chase said before slipping away. He left but made sure to look at me one last time.

Chills swept over me.

"What the fuck is he doing here?" Davian said to Rocky, who just shrugged.

"Beats me. Cerberus team is supposed to be dealing with a wolfen outbreak in the forest. I thought Chase was with them."

"Get her back to the chapter now," Davian said, referring to me. "I don't want that pig-fucker Chase to see her again. Clear?"

"Crystal sir," Rocky said.

As Rocky escorted me, he told me a little bit more about the guardians. On a regular day soldiers would work together in small groups of one or two, but they all came from a single unit that was like a family in the organization.

"Xerxes unit is the top drawer in the Guardian organization," Rocky said as we walked down gun-metal hallways. "I'm not bragging, it's just fact."

"And Davian is your leader?"

"Davian is the Commander, he used to be a field soldier himself back in the day, but now he's older he's taken on the role of a Commander. Every unit has a commander. They're sort of like a teacher. They're supposed to keep us in check. Each unit is formed with chemistry and purpose in mind. Each guardian has a unique specialty."

"And you're the tech guy?"

"That's right. Oh, take this turn here," he said, and we cut down another hallway. "Everyone in Xerxes has a specialty. Briggs can fly or drive anything. There's Charge, you met him on the landing pad. He's the explosive dude. Mac is the best in hand-to-hand combat I've ever seen, Zero is basically a fucking ninja, Hammer—"

"Hold on a second," I said. "You're running a lot of names by me here. You expect me to remember all this?"

Rocky laughed. "Sorry. I spend a lot of my time in a room alone with a computer, so I tend to ramble when we have new company. I can stop."

"No, it's okay," I laughed. "I just hope there's a chance to take notes before the main test."

"Hammer is the big guy. I know that doesn't help much when we're all this size. You can tell him apart from the rest because he's usually got a huge fucking mallet on his back. That's his weapon of choice.

"Then there's Ash. He's probably the weakest out of all of us when it comes to fighting, but he's still a unit, obviously. He's the pretty boy. He can talk his way around anything."

"Let me guess, he's the one you go to for dating advice."

"Ha," Rocky laughed. "As if I need advice. Striker is the last one. He's technically in our unit, but he's a bit of a lone wolf too. He's more of a survivalist. Likes to live on the fringe. He runs around with a fucking bow, but he's deadly with it. That's everyone."

"What about Hunter?" I asked.

"Oh, well, he's our leader."

"I thought Davian was the leader?"

"Davian is the Commander. He makes sure we don't break too many rules. Hunter answers to him and takes the blame if we step out of line. The rest of us take orders from Hunter. Anyway…. that's everyone, and this is our chapter." Rocky stopped in front of a huge metal door. A thin line ran down the middle of the door. It also divided a large emblem that had been etched into the metallic surface.

In the circle was an illustration of a musclebound figure sat atop a throne. He had a scepter in one hand and a curved blade in the other.

"Xerxes himself," I said.

"Our namesake," Rocky said. "Every unit has an individual identifier and emblem. This happens to be ours."

"The giant. The king of kings. Not exactly subtle."

Rocky shrugged and held his wrist over a keypad. "Did you get the impression anything about the guardians is subtle?"

"Fair point."

The blast doors opened to reveal a giant common room. Rocky gestured for me to step in and followed.

"This is our chapter. All units have their own living space. We have individual rooms that link around a central common area." He pointed at various corridors branching off from the large and bright room. "The only guys in here are from Xerxes unit. No dicks like Chase in here. You'd have to head down to Cerberus chapter to find him. Probably jacking off in a mirror."

"Great mental image. Thanks."

"Let me show you around," he said, and I followed Rocky into the room as he lapped the space. There were pool tables, couches, flat screen televisions, a nice kitchen, and even a couple arcade machines. It was definitely a living space shared by ten big dudes.

"Now we mostly only use the kitchen for blood, but you can put an order in with catering to get food delivered. You might want to do that if you're going to be staying here with us."

"Why are you telling me all this?" I asked as we stopped by the kitchen. "From the way you're talking you make it sound like I'm going to be here longer than a week."

Rocky turned his head and looked back at me. "I'm not sure actually, I'm just trying to be helpful. I look at you and get the impression you're sticking around. Maybe you're the girl that finally grounds Hunter." Rocky burst out laughing. "That would be something."

"Where is he? Can I see him yet?"

"No, you fucking can't," Davian said as he came around the corner. "Let me show you to your guest accommodation. I'd like you to talk us through everything that's happened so far. You'll be staying the night here while we have Hunter go through a psych debriefing to make sure he's not lost his fucking marbles. Follow me."

Davian led me to the small guest room. "The doors open with a keycard, yours is on the table there. Don't fucking lose it. You've got your own shower and there's a free laundry service. I'll get some clothes brought up for you in case you want to change. Any questions?"

"Can I shower before we sit down and talk?"

He glanced at his watch in an irritated way but nodded. "You've got twenty minutes. I'll go and grab you a change of clothes in the meantime. After that we get down to business. Clear?"

"Sir, yes, sir," I said sarcastically.

"Just what I fucking needed," Davian said as he walked out of the room. "Another smart mouth!"

Once Davian was gone, I made sure the door was locked and I undressed. I felt slightly more trusting of the guardians now, but I still had to be cautious and wouldn't relax until Hunter was back at my side.

I took the amulet with me into the bathroom and showered quickly. The hot water beat out the stress and stripped away the dirt from my body. I almost felt human again. When I was back in my room there was a knock on the door and Davian thrust a laundry basket of neatly folded clothes into my arms.

"Hurry up and dress," he growled before turning out the door. "You've got five minutes!"

I looked through the clothes and realized it was the same outfit but in three different sizes, I found mine, dried off and got dressed.

Looking at myself in the mirror I didn't see a historian, I looked like some rock-biker chick.

The outfit comprised of sleek-black trousers, which were form-fitting. There was a grey t-shirt and a leather jacket. Huge black boots finished the look. I pulled my hair up into a messy bun and contemplated asking Davian if he could issue any guardian-standard nose rings.

Something told me he wouldn't appreciate the joke.

I decided to wait outside the room to rob Davian of the satisfaction of smashing his fist against the door. He came around the corner almost as soon as I stepped into the corridor.

"About fucking time!" he growled. "Let's go!" He turned on the spot and I hurried after him.

We ended up in what looked like a small interrogation room. A metal table with four chairs was in the room's center and a one-way mirror filled the wall to my right.

Davian instructed me to sit and he sat down on the opposite side with another guardian. The guy next to him was huge—following the trend—with short blond hair, large red eyes, cut cheekbones and an almost-perfect nose.

"Name's Ash," he said and held out his hand. "You must be Hunter's mate."

"Mate?" I said as I shook hands with him. Ash and Davian just looked at one another.

"Oh. Well, I mean. Friend. The one from the museum, right?"

"Care for a coffee, Doctor Stone?" Davian asked. It was probably the most civil thing he had said to me so far. I wondered who was standing on the other side of that mirror, and if Davian was putting on a face now to butter me up for questioning.

"I'd love a coffee," I said. "Could I get a Latte?"

"What do we look like? A fucking coffee shop?" Davian began, but then he stopped himself. "I mean, of course you can get a latte, we're the goddamn guardians. Let me see if I can remember where the coffee machine is."

He left the room, leaving me alone with Ash.

"You know," he said, "I think I would have ended up as a historian or archaeologist if I didn't become a guardian."

"Really?" I asked. "You like history?"

"I know you might not think it to look at me, but I was an academic once upon a time. I didn't always look like this. Becoming a guardian changes you, physically and mentally. Would you believe I once weight 150lb and read Shakespeare in forests?"

I laughed. "No, not at all. You look more like the type that would make trouble in a bar."

Ash smiled. "More often than not that's what this job requires. What's your historical area?"

"Greek mythology has always fascinated me," I said, "but my professional career so far has specialized in ancient Chinese culture."

"I love it all," Ash said. "I've always had a fondness for ancient Egypt myself. I think a lot of people don't realize that historians like you have the most important, and maybe the hardest job. You guys don't get enough credit."

I felt myself warming at his compliment. "Well I'm not sure about that, I—"

"No, it's true," he said. "Don't you agree? The only way to plan for the future is by studying the past. The world couldn't exist without people like you, Doctor Stone. Academics like you deserve so much more credit."

"I'd never really thought of it that way, but I suppose you're right." This was strange, I had come here expecting some interrogation, but now I was floating with self-importance. Then I remembered something Rocky had told me on our walk over here.

"Then there's Ash. He's probably the weakest out of all of us when it comes to fighting, but he's still a unit, obviously. He's the pretty boy. He can talk his way around anything."

"Ah," I said to myself. "The pretty boy. You're charming me."

Ash smiled and sat back in his chair, acting like he was surprised. "I don't know what you're talking about."

"You're *so* into ancient Egypt, right? Can you tell me the name of an emperor?"

"Uh… Cleopatra?"

"Anyone else?"

Ash drummed his fingers on the metal table before laughing. "Okay, fuck. You got me. I'm just trying to make you feel at ease. If Davian had his way, we'd both be playing bad cop."

Davian came back into the room then. He put a cup of black coffee on the table, sat down and pulled out a cigar.

"Machine's broken," he grunted. "Shall we begin? I'd like you to talk us through everything that's happened so far."

I started at the beginning, being the point when Harkin had opened the tomb and Hunter dropped down through the ceiling. I left out a few details, namely the parts where we had fucked, but for the most part I told him the truth.

Davian and Ash just listened, for which I was grateful. It felt good to get everything off my chest.

"What about the amulet?" Ash said as I finally caught up to the present moment. "How are you getting on with that?"

"I've heard Halo's guidance a few times. It told me to throw the amulet at those bikers and then it exploded with light. Then it told me to trust Davian and the guardians."

Davian looked surprised; Ash just laughed. "Damn," Ash said. "Maybe we should question Halo's judge of character?"

"Go fuck yourself, soldier," Davian said. "Did Hunter explain how the amulet works? That it's a way to find Halo's hiding place?"

"He did, but I haven't been able to figure anything out so far. "Should I—" I reached into my pocket to pull the amulet out when Davian stopped me.

"No!" he shouted. "What the fuck did I tell you about pulling that thing out around us? There's no telling how we'll react."

"Sorry, I thought it would be helpful."

"Keep it to yourself for now," Davian reminded me. He looked at Ash and then at the mirrored wall. "I think we've got everything we need for now. We'll see if your story syncs with Hunter's. If he passes his psych evaluation tonight, you'll both be reunited tomorrow." Davian stood up from the table and Ash followed suit. I joined them.

"That's everything?" I asked. "What do I do now?"

"Ash will escort you back to your room. You're to stay there until we finish with Hunter."

"What happens if he doesn't pass your tests?"

Davian turned and looked at me solemnly. "We'll get you a new guardian, someone that will keep you safe."

The commander went to leave before I shouted after him. "Davian. Stop!" He did, but he didn't look all the way back. "Why do I get the feeling you're not telling me everything?"

Davian did look back now. He glanced at the mirror and then at me.

"This isn't the first time Hunter's been involved with the amulet," he said. "He was there the last time it was found, and it went pretty fucking badly."

8

HUNTER

I came to in a room with very little light, strapped to a metal chair with iron chains running around my body. I was still in my birthday suit.

Saydra was standing about ten feet in front of me, she was wearing long black flowing robes. I also saw the silhouette of a guardian behind her. It could be difficult to tell my brothers apart sometimes when they were in full gear, but I knew this wasn't a guardian from my chapter, so, who was it?

I could just make out the faint emblem of a skull on his left breast-plate. It meant this guardian was a member of the Black Skulls, one of the most deranged fucking units in the entire organization. They were the guys we sent into handle the jobs that no one else wanted.

I cleared my throat.

"A guy wakes up in a room and sees a psychic witch and a Black Skull. He'd shit his pants, but they didn't give him any," I joked before adopting a more serious tone. "What the fuck is going on here Saydra, and why have you got…" I squinted at the silhouette again. "Gavrilo here with you?"

Gavrilo made the slightest of involuntary movements, indicating that it was in fact, him. Pretty much every guardian in the organization was terrified of Gavrilo. He had a reputation for being a master torturer. The guardian would do anything to get the answers he needed, far surpassing the limits that stopped others.

He didn't bother me at all, but I found it very interesting that Saydra had chosen to bring him here for backup.

That wasn't like Saydra at all.

"We need to make sure your mind hasn't been warped," Saydra said. "We need to know the amulet hasn't taken your conscious and turned it dark."

"And you intend to find that out by torturing me?"

"Gavrilo isn't here to torture you. He's here to kill you, should you ask him to do so. He was the only one that would take the call."

I nodded slowly. "I understand what is happening now," I said. "You're going to sweep my mind."

Saydra's face didn't show emotion. I wasn't sure the psychic vampire witch was even capable of feeling emotions. The deep and endless glossiness of her eyes changed slightly though, suggesting that she regretted the decision.

"That is right."

That explained why Gavrilo was here. A sweep was an incredibly painful psychic interrogation, and it left most begging for death. If things went wrong the pain was irreversible and never-ending.

That's where Gavrilo came in.

The fucker didn't bother me in the slightest, but I had to admit his unwavering gaze could be slightly unnerving at times. Most feared him, but I had done jobs with him in the past and I could see his heart was in the right place, even if his methods were sometimes questionable.

"I was getting ready to kill you," I said to Gavrilo. "I guess I should be thanking you." He nodded back at me simply. The faceless assassin wasn't one for many words. "Your services won't be required though. So, go."

He and Saydra looked at one another. She glanced at me.

"You're sure?" Saydra asked.

"Yep," I said. I'm not dying here, and you're not fucking this up, so he's not necessary. You can go."

The silent behemoth left the room. Saydra's face did not change.

"Are the chains necessary?" I asked.

"Most go completely catatonic when subjected to a sweep," she said. "But you... you don't. Last time this happened you nearly killed me. The chains are for my safety."

"The girl tried to give me the amulet. I refused it."

"I suspect you're telling me the truth," the witch said. "But the organization wants to make sure. Shall we get this over with?"

I took in a deep breath of air and readied myself. All the years of training, mutilation, surgery and modifications... it was all hell on earth, but it was nothing compared to a mind-sweep from Saydra. I'd been here once before and it was the most intense pain and suffering I'd ever felt.

When I was last here, I could barely remember a single thing when it was over. They had twelve guardians in the room, and it took all twelve of them to tear me away from Saydra. The sweep had nearly broken my mind, and my body had taken over to defend itself. It had planned to rip her limb from limb.

"Everyone thought you'd betrayed the guardians last time the amulet was found," Saydra said. "Once I looked in your mind, we saw the truth. Trey was the one that betrayed us, not you."

"And I killed him," I said.

My best friend.

The guy I'd grown up with.

We'd known each other since kids. We were turned by the same maker, taken in by the same recruiter. We walked through the fires of the forge together and stood by one another. I wouldn't have survived without him, and he wouldn't have survived without me.

Once we graduated, we were inseparable. The two of us were a well-oiled machine. No one else could match our case rate. For years we were untouchable, but then a case landed in our laps and it changed everything for good.

A girl had found the Halo Amulet, and Saydra had assigned Trey to guard her. I was his backup. I knew from the offset that something wasn't right, but I ignored the feeling. The girl wasn't just some nobody, she turned out to be Trey's mate, and I was fucking ecstatic for him.

Things turned south when we found Halo, however.

The journey ended in a burial mound in Ireland. Lauriel, Trey's mate and the chosen keeper, was about to return the amulet when Trey up and killed her. The amulet had corrupted him. I had no choice but to take his life. I plunged a stake through his chest and watched my best friend turn to ash.

"You still never told me what you wished for," Saydra said, holding her hand a few inches away from my temple. "I couldn't see the answer, even when I looked into your mind."

"Conditions of a contract," I said. "I swore I'd never tell. Can we get this over with already?"

Without another word she placed her hand against my head.

As the witch's fingers grazed my skin the most blinding pain swept through my body, igniting every nerve with the fire of agony and suffering. Cursed roaring filled the interrogation room and my body flung back to try and be anywhere but here.

There were bolts keeping the metal chair to the floor, but I could hear the metal twisting and straining under my thrashing. A million images flashed before my eyes like pages from a book, each one a razor-sharp knife stabbing into my brain.

Beyond the images I saw the face of Saydra.

Her eyes were all white and her hair floated up from the floor as purple electricity crackled all around us. She held her hand steadfast against my forehead despite my constant thrashing. Her psychic power crashed through every corridor of my brain, crushing every neuron and burning every synapse.

She was basically forcing me into a grand mal seizure. I was expected to hold on while I ignored the phantom sensations of suffering. Invisible tacks slammed through my fingernails. My spinal column felt as though it twisted like a wet-towel and crumbled to dust. A million tiny knives were peeling away tiny slivers of my skin.

I had no idea how long it lasted, but it finished with me slumped forward and sitting completely still. In the few seconds that followed there was only the sound of climatic silence.

My head heavy, I managed to look up and saw Saydra lying on the floor about five feet back from her starting position. Purple electricity continued to crackle over her body as her eyes faded back to black. Steam curled up from my body. Every muscle screamed with the fatigue of exhaustion.

"Well?" I managed. "Am I free to go or not?"

"You're clear," she said after a very long pause. "My earlier visions were correct. You're the only one that can see this through."

Saydra waved her hand and the heavy chains keeping me in place dropped to the floor like iron gauntlets. I stood up very slowly and stretched out my aching bones. The sweep was over now, but the witch hadn't got up from the floor and the look in her eye told me that something was wrong.

"What does that mean?" I asked. "See it through? Why are you looking at me like that?" For the first time in my life I saw vulnerability in her eyes. It frightened me. "Answer me witch! Has the amulet corrupted me or not!"

She pushed her weight onto her elbows and regained a little of her composure. "The purpose of my sweep was to see if you're the one who can get this job done. Whether or not you're corrupted is no longer my concern."

"What are you trying to say? That I'm going to betray Rachel?"

Not in a million years.

"I'm saying that when the time comes, whatever you end up doing, it doesn't matter. All that matters is that you are there. I can't tell you what will happen, Hunter, that's not how this works."

I clenched my fist tight. "I'm not going to betray her."

"You're going to get the job done, that's all I can say. And that's all that matters."

"I'm done with this bullshit. Are we done here?"

The witch nodded. "Are you going to see her, next?"

"Your sister?" I asked.

Saydra nodded again. "Yes."

"She's the only one that can tell us how to work this thing, so yeah. I guess so."

"Things are different this time," Saydra said. "Nalinth, she has changed. Her powers are darker and far greater than mine. She will try to kill you this time, Hunter. One will have to die to leave."

"I guess I'll be killing your sister then."

She shook her head, her black eyes full and somehow empty. "Not possible. There's only one other option."

"I don't want to hear it," I said. "We're done. I don't want to see you again."

I was clear to go back to Rachel as soon as I'd passed Saydra's sweep. I left the witch in the interrogation room. There was nothing else I wanted to say to her. Outside I found Commander Davian waiting for me in the hallway. He passed me a black gown, I put it on, and we started walking in silence.

"How was it?" he asked, a fresh cigar burning away in his mouth.

"Like two weeks in Fiji, how do you think?"

He laughed slightly. "The higherups didn't give me any choice, I told them you'd pass."

"Where's the girl?"

"In the guest wing of the chapter. I expect she's asleep by now. What did Saydra say?"

"The same cryptic bullshit she usually says," I scowled. "She might need help getting out of there, I think it was harder on her than me."

We turned onto the main corridor which lead back to our chapter. "She'll be fine," Davian growled. "She does this shit several times a year. I'll put the whole unit on this moving forward. You get all the resources and backup you need. No questions asked."

"No," I shook my head. "Saydra made it pretty clear that I've got to tackle this on my own. Any other arrangement will fuck things up."

"Hunter listen," Davian said as he came to a stop. I already knew what was coming next. "Is this like last time? Do you need to go and see *her* again?"

The *her* he was referring to was Nalinth, Saydra's dark sister and Davian's ex-lover.

"She was the only one that could help us last time, I suspect nothing has changed."

"You've done this once before," he said. "Don't you know how to use the amulet by now?"

"Lauriel was the keeper last time, not me," I reminded him. "I was just there to help keep her alive, and I failed."

"That was Trey's fault, not yours."

"I guess we remember it differently."

"Let me go with you," he said. "To Nalinth. I can talk sense into her, make sure she doesn't do anything stupid."

"She's not the same woman you fell in love with Davian. You'd still be together if that much was true. Coming with us is only going to get you killed and we both know it."

"She listens to me. I can get through to her, I can keep you safe."

"With all due respect, shove it up your ass, sir. You're better off staying here and we both know it. Now if you'll excuse me, I have to go and collapse in a bed next to my mate, I'm hanging on by a thread here."

I left Davian in the hallway and made my way back to the chapter. When I got there, I headed straight for the guest wing and knocked on the occupied room. A few seconds passed before the door slid open to reveal Rachel.

"Hunter?!" she gasped, jumping forward to throw her arms around me. It was the best welcome I'd ever received, though the pain in my body made it hard to catch her.

"I knew you'd miss me," I winced. She quickly pulled back.

"Are you hurt? Did they hurt you?"

"Not like that," I said. "Did I wake you?"

"Barely. I only just drifted off."

"Mind if I come in and crash? My rooms at the opposite end of the chapter and I'm not sure I can make it that far."

"Terrible line, but come on in."

I went straight for the bed and crashed on my back, letting out a long sigh at having made it. Rachel locked the door behind her and nestled in beside me. It felt damn good to have her back at my side.

"You look completely spent," she said. "Are you sure you're okay?"

"Nothing a little sleep won't fix," I said, pulling her in tight against my body. "You smell good. Did you shower?"

"I did. Maybe I can help you get cleaned up in the morning."

"Sounds good to me," I said, laughing to myself.

Though exhausted, sleep didn't come to me straight away. It wasn't long before Rachel dozed off beside me. I was left with my thoughts, staring up at the slate-grey ceiling and wondering what Saydra's words had meant.

Would I betray Rachel like Trey betrayed Lauriel?

Would I kill my own mate with the promise of eternal power?

"No," I growled to myself, the words rumbling like a deep fire in the pit of my chest.

I'd rather die first.

9

RACHEL

Sleeping next to Hunter was equal parts difficult and amazing. It's was so easy to cozy up next to him and feel completely safe, I hadn't slept this well in ages. Having my leg draped over his powerful thighs was incredibly arousing however and keeping myself off him was a challenge in itself.

Somehow, I managed.

I was tired myself and it was pretty clear that Hunter had nothing left in the tank. I didn't know what had happened during his psych evaluation, but he was a ghost on his feet when he came back to my room.

When I woke up in the morning, I found him stirring at the same time as me. I kissed him on the shoulder, and he kissed my forehead.

"Morning," I said. "How are you feeling now?"

"A lot better," he said with a deep groan. We both sat up together. He still looked a bit stiff, but it was a definite improvement on the man I'd seen last night.

"Can I get you a drink? Will blood make you feel better?"

He nodded. "Please. There's a tap on the wall over there. If you could fill a glass and bring it over, that would go a long way in repairing me."

I hopped out of bed and skipped across the room to the small kitchenette. Three faucets hung over a small basin. There was a blue dot on one, a red on the other and the third was black.

"The black one," Hunter said from the bed behind me.

I grabbed a glass and held it under the right faucet. The sight of dark red liquid took me by surprise as it gushed out and filled the glass. Where did it come from exactly? Did they have a killing floor somewhere within the HQ? I hoped it wasn't something as macabre as that, but this was going to take some getting used to.

I walked back over to Hunter. He took the glass, thanked me, and downed the drink in one.

"It's synthetic," he said after taking a breath.

"Pardon me?" I asked.

"The blood. You're wondering where it comes from."

"Oh well..." I laughed. "I was. Are you always reading my thoughts now?"

"I can't help it. Our bond is getting stronger and I'll naturally pick up your thoughts to make sure your needs are being met."

"Is that normal for a guardian?" My voice strained a little as I asked the question. I think Hunter got the point. I could tell that our relationship was far from normal.

"You're asking me what this is..." he said, pointing between himself and me.

"Someone used the word 'mate' last night," I said. I hadn't been able to forget the word since hearing it. I had to cut to the chase.

Hunter nodded to himself, looking like he was gearing up to tell me something.

"Vampires are different from humans," he said. "You know that much."

"Okay."

"Well, our mating process is different too. I mean, we fuck like humans, but we do it better."

"Naturally."

Guardians sure had a way with words.

"But uh, actually finding a *mate*, the one you're meant to be with? That's different for vampires."

"Different how?" I asked, crossing my arms.

"It's not just a feeling for us. It's an empirical truth that beats through the fiber of our soul. Each vampire has *one* mate, one person that they're *meant* to be with, and we *know* when we find them."

"Okay…"

"You're my mate, Rachel," he said. "You're my one. I should have told you earlier. I'm sorry. I knew it from the moment I set eyes on you."

"This is all a bit insane," I said. Hunter laughed, which made me laugh. I wasn't expecting that reaction. "Why are you laughing?"

"Because you're absolutely right. It's completely insane. But I have to be honest with you now, that is how I feel and that is what you mean to me. I have found you now, and I can never unfind you. You have left your mark upon my soul, and that mark can never be taken away."

"I'm still getting my head around this. I was single a few days ago. I mean, I *am* single. Now I'm supposed to commit to one guy for ever and ever, amen? Oh, and he's a vampire?"

"Look I know I'm supposed to tell you that you can walk away, and you have a choice, but let's be honest, that's all bullshit."

"Is it now?" I said, crossing my arms over my chest.

The giant vampire stood up from the bed and approached me. Walking with a swagger that belayed absolute confidence. "Yeah, because there's no fucking way I'm letting you get away from me, and there's not a chance in hell that I'm taking no for an answer." He stopped in front of me, his huge body brushing up against the front of mine. My throat went tight and I forgot how to breathe.

"From the sounds of things there's more you haven't told me," I said, turning away from him.

"Oh?"

I walked over to the cabinet where I had stashed the amulet and pulled it out, holding it up so Hunter could see it. "You were around last time this was found. Davian told me."

"I see," he said.

"Why didn't you tell me about this? It seems like a pretty crucial piece of info to leave out. You said that no one knows who made the last wish, and now I learn you were there? What happened exactly?"

Hunter let out a long sigh.

"I killed my best friend," he said. The answer took me by surprise.

"What?"

"Trey. He was my partner in the guardians. More than a partner. A brother. We grew up together. He was my shadow my whole life. Well... a girl found the amulet in 1883. Her name was Lauriel. Trey and I were assigned to look after her, and what would you know, she turned out to be Trey's mate."

"Wait," I said. "1883? How old are you?"

"I stopped aging when I became a vampire," Hunter explained. "I was born in 1801. If you were counting by human years, then that would make me 219. Biologically I'm still in my thirties."

There was so much I still didn't know about Hunter's vampirism. It was amazing to me that someone could live that long and look so... great.

"So you were around when Krakatoa last erupted?"

"Yep. The ever dark was the same last time around."

"And this girl, this Lauriel, she was the keeper, like I am now?"

"Yup," he nodded. "Lauriel learned to use the amulet and we found Halo's hiding place, but when we got there things went horribly wrong. Trey killed her, and he tried to take the amulet for himself. The amulet had consumed his mind, and the draw of absolute power had taken him in. I was left with no choice but to kill him."

"Hunter I'm... I'm sorry."

"Don't be. With the clock ticking I could let the amulet disappear or make a wish. Letting it disappear wasn't an option, so I took the wish. It was me. I was the last one."

"What did you wish for?" I said, enraptured by the story.

He looked away. "I can't say. I made a deal with Halo. That was part of it."

"A deal?" I asked. "What deal?"

"Rachel," he said sternly. "I can't."

"Okay. Sorry. What now then? If you've done this before it can't be that hard to find her again?"

Hunter shook his head. "The hunt is different every time. That's all I can say. Last time we had to employ someone to help us, and I'm afraid we'll have to ask that person again."

"Who?"

"Her name is Nalinth. She is a dark witch, and sister to Saydra, the witch that receives visions for the guardians. She's also Davian's ex."

"This Nalinth, is she dangerous?"

"Extremely, and if Saydra's predictions are right then Nalinth has only got more dangerous."

"Can't Saydra help us?"

"No. She doesn't understand how the amulet works. Look we're on day three here. We've got four days left until the sun goes out forever. I don't exactly want to go back to this crazy vampire bitch, but we haven't got a choice."

"Let's go then," I said. "If worst comes to worst then Halo will protect us from this Nalinth."

"There's just a small matter of finding her," Hunter said. "And that's where you come in."

"Me? How should I know where she is?"

He gestured to the amulet in my hand. "With that. That's how Lauriel found her last time. Hold the amulet up, look in the stone, and ask for help. Ask to find Nalinth."

"I… it can't be that easy. Right?"

"Trust me," Hunter said. "Nothing about this is going to be easy."

I glanced at him for a moment before taking the amulet out of the cloth. I walked over and sat down on the bed before holding up the stone. The green gem turned on the chain and twinkled in the room's light. It was oddly hypnotic, like waves crashing against a beach, or flames dancing over a burning fire.

As I looked into the stone It seemed like all the sound in the world was slowly fading out. A gentle ringing sound whistled in the distance and started to grow louder. The chain felt taut in my hand. My eyes were drawn to the stone, like a wave of magnetic energy was keeping my attention in place.

I felt as though I was leaning forward, or sinking in the middle of a giant lake, a stone plummeting down into cold and icy depths. My periphery faded to black, it was just me and the stone now. A voice echoed in the distance. It was Halo.

What do you want?

"How do I find you?" I asked. "How do I use the amulet?" In the stone I saw a face appear. It was an elfin-featured girl with beautiful golden hair. "Halo?" I asked.

Find Nalinth. She will guide you there.

"Where is she?"

A church of bones. Blood on the river.

Images swam in my vision to accompany her words.

I saw swamps and bayou. Spanish moss dangled over still water. Twisted trees curled into night like broken fingers. Fire burned on a black lake. A huge wooden church stood tall among the trees, a dark tower against a night of fire. I saw boats, I saw bones. I saw flames.

The water was black. A cursed mirror.

The vision broke and I felt the trance end. I heard myself gasp and then realized I was falling backwards.

"Rachel!" Hunter shouted, his strong arms wrapping around me as he caught me. "Rachel? What happened? What did you see?"

It felt bizarre to be back in the room. It was like a dream had just ended and thrown me back into a world I had forgotten about. "Trees," I said. "Bayou. Swamp. I think Nalinth is meant to be there somewhere."

"That's hardly narrowing it down, darling," Hunter laughed. "What else did you see?"

"A church. All tall and painted black. The wood was carved. It looked almost like a cathedral. I saw boats, I saw fire... I saw bones."

"Voodoo," Hunter said to himself. "Nalinth must have taken up residence as a voodoo priestess, that kind of thing is right up her alley."

"You know where she is?" I asked.

"No, but I reckon someone that might. Bayou. Voodoo. I'd put my money on Louisiana. I've got an informant down there; he might be able to point us in the right direction."

"All we have to do is avoid the bad guys and find Halo, right?" I said. "It can't be that hard. Is Harkin still a threat?"

"Harkin is *the* threat," Hunter said. "Any vampire that learns about this amulet will probably want a piece of us. "Luckily for us Harkin has no way of getting in here. He doesn't know where the guardian HQ is and even if he did it's a fortress of—"

Hunter's words stopped dead in his mouth as a distant rumbling sound shook through the room. "What the fuck was that?" he muttered to himself.

The rumble was followed immediately by the muted clatter of gunfire, which I never thought I would be able to identify before this week. I heard guardians shouting in the common room outside, screaming orders over the gunfire.

"Hunter? What's going on!" I asked.

"I think the powers of your amulet are starting to come into play," Hunter said. "But they're working against us."

"Back down!" a voice shouted outside the corridor. "Back down!"

"Where are they? Give them up!" another muffled voice shouted.

Suddenly a small screen came to life on the interior wall by the door. Rocky's face filled the monitor. "Hey! Anyone order a wakeup call?"

"What's going on out there?" Hunter said to Rocky.

"So, Chase from Cerberus unit has turned on us—"

"No surprises there," Hunter growled.

"He's just blown open the door to our unit and he's got a mech-suit. Oh, also he's with like ten other guys and they're all in mech-suits too."

"Harkin's guys by any chance?"

"I haven't got an ID on them yet, but I'd put my money on it. You've got about fifteen seconds before they break down that door."

"Chase must have let Harkin's guys in. That means he's working with Harkin. Have you got an exit strategy for us?"

"Hey, it's me, Rocky. Of course, I do! I'm about to slam the common room with an EMP. That will take out the mech-suits."

"But it also means you won't be able to communicate with us."

Rocky clicked his fingers and pointed at the camera. "Bingo. So, I'll have to unload a bunch of instructions on you right now. All guest rooms have a secret weapons cache. Punch the ceiling panel directly above your head."

Hunter did so.

The ceiling panel dropped through the air, along with a metallic briefcase that had been hidden above it. Hunter caught the case, crouched down and opened it to reveal a huge shotgun and two hand-guns. All the weapons had huge clips sticking out of them.

"Do you know how to fire a gun?" he said and threw a handgun to me. He tucked the other into his waistband and grabbed the shotgun, immediately taking point as he aimed it at the door.

"I guess we're about to find out," I said, though I'd never even held a gun before.

"Lock your arms and keep your feet apart. Only aim at something if you want to kill it. Congratulations, firearm initiation over."

"Eight seconds," Rocky said. "Listen and don't talk, because there's no time. You have to get out of guardian HQ right away. Take Rachel and the amulet with you. Don't come back until the mission is done. You're going to take a left when you get out the room. Head for the maintenance tunnels underneath the common room and then head for sanitation.

"I stashed a vehicle there for situations like this. Take it to get wherever you're going. Contact me when you're back online."

"What about you?" Hunter asked, his gun still trained on the door.

"Don't worry about me. I always come out on top. I'm dropping the EMP now. Bye!"

I expected a huge explosion, but the reality is that everything electrical immediately died a death. The lights went out and the room plunged into darkness. The pace of the commotion shifted outside and then the gunfire continued.

Hunter looked over his shoulder at me and smiled.

"Get ready Doctor Stone," he said with a note of excitement in his voice. "This might get a little hairy."

The door to the guest room exploded open and Hunter fired his shotgun. I squeezed my finger against my trigger and hoped for the best.

Mayhem had started.

10

HUNTER

The shotgun exploded in my hands, wiping out the vampire that had blown down the door. The cloud of pellet shrapnel tore through the air and made mincemeat of his chest, instantly turning him into a ball of screaming flame.

I pumped the chamber to reload and two more figures came around the corner. Rachel's gun went off, nailing one of them square in the head. I was impressed, my crash-course firearms initiation had obviously been effective.

The headshot sent the second vampire up in flames, and I took out the last one with another blast from my shotgun.

"Stay close!" I shouted to Rachel as I ran to the door. A quick check revealed that the hallway immediately outside was clear, but as soon as we stepped out the action caught up to us.

Guardian HQ's sleek gunmetal hallways were now bathed in dim red light from the emergency lighting system. The common room was to our right, where I saw Hammer and Mac holding off a group of Harkin's men. Hammer was swinging his giant fucking mallet around and making quick work of the minions, while Mac was using the deadliest weapons he had available: his bare hands.

Throughout the surrounding hallways I could hear the theatre of combat and gunfire coming from all directions. We just had to follow Rocky's instructions and get out of there alive. I wanted to stay and help my brothers, but that wasn't an option right now.

"Mac!" Hammer shouted while dealing with three minions at once. "Watch out!"

Mac had no problem dealing with idiots like this, Harkin's goons weren't trained fighters and couldn't match the speed or strength of a guardian, but this was a surprise attack, they had numbers, and they fought dirty.

One of the downed goons had found a pistol on the floor and had it aimed at the back of Mac's head while he was facing another direction.

Fucking coward.

With a flash of my hand I whipped out the handgun tucked into my waistband and nailed the fucker. The gun dropped to the floor as he burst into flame.

Both Hammer and Mac looked down the hallway to trace the shot and saw me with Rachel. "Hunter!" Mac shouted. "Run!"

Saving Mac's life had drawn unnecessary attention to us, but I wasn't about to let my brother die to one of Harkin's goons. I temporarily holstered the shotgun and flung Rachel over my shoulder as I burst down the corridor, heading away from the common room. Looking back, I saw my guardian brothers fighting off the advancing hoard, giving us time to get away.

There was a small section at the back of the chapter set aside for maintenance. A long tunnel ran down the back of the communal living space and led down to basements with washers and dryers. There was also a service elevator that went straight up to a private flight deck.

It would have been my escape route, and it was the one I'd laid out in my head before talking to Rocky, but as we came around the corner, I realized why he'd suggested an alternative. Chase, the guardian that had betrayed us, was standing in front of the elevator with another group of Harkin's goons. Large mech-suits were scattered across the floor, rendered useless by Rocky's EMP.

"There!" one of the goons shouted as I came around the corner. They all instantly pointed their rifles in our direction. The maintenance tunnels were directly past the service elevator, if we wanted to get out of there, we needed to somehow get past Chase and his men.

"Lower your weapons!" Chase shouted to the goons, sounding like he was in a hot panic. "We need the girl alive!"

I kept my own weapon pointed directly at the group, but a solitary shotgun was little fucking use against ten vampires with assault rifles. I could probably withstand the brunt of their fire, but it would only take one bullet to kill Rachel, and I wasn't going to take that risk.

The goons followed Chase's orders. "It's over Hunter," he barked at me. "Hand the girl over."

"Not on your fucking life."

"Don't make me risk her," he said. "I will tell them to shoot if you don't cooperate."

I wasn't going to stand there and bargain with Chase over Rachel's life. Turning on the guardians was already a big fucking indicator that his mind wasn't making rational decisions, I couldn't be sure he valued her life over his own insanity.

"Put me down," Rachel whispered in my ear. "I have an idea."

"Can you throw the amulet again?" I asked.

"Better than that."

I set her down and she turned around to face the group. "You need me alive," she said to Chase.

"Without the keeper the amulet is pretty fucking useless, so yeah—you're a necessity."

"Then how about we make things a little fairer?" she said. Her next act caught all of us by surprise. She pulled out her handgun and pointed it at her head. "Let us past or I blow my fucking brains out!"

"Rachel!" I shouted.

"Christ!" Chase shouted, shaking his head in disbelief. "She's the fucking craziest one here!"

"Drop your weapons now, all of you," she said to the group. "If you don't let us past, I'll pull the trigger, and then you all lose."

"Do it!" Chase said. "Fucking do it!"

"Fuck that," one of the goons said. "Harkin's orders were very clear. Get the amulet. The girl is optional. And you," he looked at Chase and pointed his gun at him. "You are just as expendable."

"What the fuck did you say?" Chase said, his brow turning down with anger. "You're not getting out of here without me, so remember who you're talking to!"

The group was turning in on themselves, which was good, but it still didn't give us a way past, and Rachel still had a gun pressed against her head. I had no idea how to get past Chase and Harkin's men, but the answer presented itself. The unexpected solution came screaming down the hallway in the form of a rocket-propelled grenade.

The missile exploded in the middle of the group, filling the corridor with fire, debris, and bodies. I grabbed hold of Rachel and pulled her around the corner just in time to avoid the wall of fire, throwing my body over hers as a human shield.

Fragments of tile and concrete rained down on my back. After a few seconds I sat up and snatched the handgun from her. "What the fuck were you thinking?!"

"I was distracting them; I wasn't really going to shoot myself. Davian was behind them, didn't you see?"

I pulled Rachel up and kept tight hold of her hand as I looked back around the corner. A charred crater now stood where the group had been. The explosion had wiped them out completely. Davian was jogging down the corridor with an RPG on his shoulder. Charge and Zero were with him.

"You motherfuckers all right?" Davian said to me and Rachel.

"Yeah, I owe you one," I said. "Rocky's plotted us an escape route. We're getting out. We know were Nalinth is."

"Good. I've got to take the boys and head to the pod. Caleb wasn't the only one to turn, his whole fucking unit went south. They've launched synchronized attacks across all of HQ."

"Scatter attack? It's a distraction," I said.

A classic battle tactic. Hit your enemy with lots of small attacks to confuse them. It suggested there was more than one target.

But what?

"Saydra," Davian said. "Rachel and the amulet weren't the only target. They're going for her too."

That made a lot of sense. If Harkin got his hands on our psychic witch that could put him at a massive advantage.

Another explosion rumbled somewhere in the belly of HQ, followed by showers of distant gunfire. The action was coming back towards us, whatever direction it was coming from.

"Go!" Davian screamed at us as he started down the hallway. "Get out of here and solve this thing, Hunter! If you guys fuck this up the whole world is over!"

"Like I need reminding!" I growled.

We went our separate ways, me hoisting Rachel over my shoulder again as I went down to maintenance and followed the signs for sanitation. In a few minutes we were tearing down dark tunnelways that ran underneath the complex, listening to the sounds of warfare overhead.

The tunnel came to an end at an abandoned delivery dock which backed onto an old lake. The dock itself was a wide concrete shelf cut into the building's exterior. Rocky's ship was hidden underneath a large tarp. It was an Xexos-4, a small experimental ship used by the guardians. The sleek black ship was glassy and smooth, and just big enough for two people.

Rachel and I quickly jumped in and I started up the controls. Her seat was directly behind mine.

"Don't we need a runway?!" she shouted.

"No need!" I shouted back, hitting the vertical thrusters to lift the jet off the ground. The engines roared all around us, amplified by the small concrete shelf the jet had been hiding on. As soon as the engines had reached full capacity, I thrust them forward and the ship took off like a rocket across the lake. I brought her up into the air and on the rear-image I saw HQ quickly slip into the distance.

The many buildings were hidden amongst trees and hills, and as we flew towards the clouds, I saw fire covering the land. Harkin had hit us with everything he had, and the attack was devastating.

Once we reached cruising altitude the ship's navigations systems turned on properly.

"Welcome," a female voice said across the cabin. "Please state your destination."

"Louisiana. HQ approved landing strips only."

The guardians had private hangars hidden all across the country, so we always had somewhere to stash our state-of-the-art jets when moving across state lines.

"One hangar found in Louisiana. Estimated flight time of two hours. Engage auto-pilot?"

"Confirmed," I said, loosening my grip as the controls took on a life of their own. With my hands free I turned my chair around to face Rachel. "Pulling a gun on yourself, seriously?"

"It worked didn't it?" she shrugged.

"Your safety is the number one priority, and you directly disobeyed that. I have to admit it though... we wouldn't have got out of there without your quick thinking."

She smiled back at me knowingly. "So, I'm off the hook then?"

I laughed. "Oh, far from it. As soon as we land, we're finding a safehouse. You've got a bad streak in you, and I need to set the record straight. That little behind of yours will be sore for days."

Rachel just tongued her cheek. "Bring it big boy."

11

RACHEL

It was just after midday when we landed in Louisiana, but thanks to the ever dark it still looked like the middle of the night. The jet's autopilot handled most of the flight, only requiring Hunter to take the controls again when it came to the landing.

We came down on an abandoned plot of tarmac somewhere in the middle of nowhere. The runway looked like it hadn't been used in years, a small private airstrip probably set aside for millionaires and sports stars that had moved to the country to get away from the city.

A long row of deserted hangers sat at the top of the strip. The jet took back control and steered itself into a black hangar, the broad doors opening automatically as we approached. Hunter informed me the guardians had secret supply caches all over the country, and this small hanger was one of them.

There was already another jet inside, several flashy sports cars and some bigger off-road vehicles too. Hunter and I climbed out of the jet. He helped me down and I followed him into a small office set in the rear corner of the hangar. A large map of the area filled the wall over a commanding corner desk. To our right were floor-to-ceiling lockers.

Hunter sat in a swivel-chair and logged into a laptop sitting on the table.

"What are you doing?" I asked as he scrolled through complicated looking screens.

"Gearing up. We need accommodation, a vehicle, weapons and provisions. I'm checking out the inventory."

"Just make sure we get a motel with AC," I groaned. I couldn't bear the thought of Louisiana heat without AC.

Hunter laughed and got up from the table as one of the lockers opened behind us. He pulled out an automatic rifle, a large black duffle bag and a set of keys.

"Motels? Come on. We're past that now," he said, quickly walking out of the office and back into the hangar.

I ran after him.

"What does that mean?!" I shouted. One of the flashy black sports cars in front of us unlocked and Hunter threw the stuff into the trunk. He looked at me.

"The guardians have safe houses and supply caches all over the country. It ensures our agents are always well supplied, regardless of our location. I've booked us into a nice little cabin just a few miles from here. Once we've unpacked our things, we'll go find my contact." He opened the driver door and smiled. "Hop in. Let's go for a spin."

I climbed in the car and buckled up as the vampire turned the engine on. It sounded like a lion had just walked in.

"What is this thing anyway?" I shouted over the roaring engine. "It's loud!"

"Bugatti Veyron!" Hunter shouted back over the din. He pressed the pedal down and let the engine roar again. "Top speed of 250mph!"

I laughed nervously.

"Well, we're obviously not driving that fast," I said.

"Oh, Rachel," Hunter said as he shifted the car into gear. "You haven't seen me drive yet."

We burst out of the hangar like a bullet from a gun, the car screaming across the tarmac as Hunter pulled into a long skid. I threw my hands out and grabbed hold of anything I could, wailing as he gunned it into the night.

I shot daggers at the vampire, who simply beamed back at me as he laughed. The car pulled off the airstrip and onto proper roads. Hunter put his foot down and sped up.

"Come on!" he shouted. "It's fun!"

"Oh, for sure!" I had to admit it was a *little* fun. "My mind is just preoccupied with other things."

"Like what?!"

"I'm wondering if Halo would send another guardian to protect me if I kill you."

"Very funny," Hunter said.

"Who said anything about joking?"

We bolted down country roads, zooming across the bayou until Hunter finally pulled off the main road and turned onto a more desolate track. Rows of silver birches bordered a long and winding gravel drive, which led up to a contemporary looking estate that wouldn't be out of a place in a modern architecture magazine.

My mouth dropped as I got out of the car and gawped at the building.

"Are you fucking serious?" I said.

"Were you expecting something else?" Hunter said, smirking as he pulled our things out of the car.

"I don't know, a little wooden shack or something. That's what comes to mind when I think 'cabin.'"

"We do have properties like that in our catalog," he said. We ascended tall stairs that led up to the property front. Once there he scanned his wrist over a keypad and the doors swung open. "I prefer the fancier stuff though. Got to keep little miss princess happy."

"*I'm* the princess?" We stepped inside and I found myself in an elaborate hallway with a grand staircase. "You guardians run around acting like super-mutant jocks but then you sneak back to the lap of luxury. Spritzing yourself with fine colognes, racing around in sportscars, drying yourself with fine Egyptian cotton."

"More often than not our work requires infiltration of high society. A lot of scrupulous paranormal activity takes place there." Hunter set the bags down and started up the stairs, gesturing for me to follow him. "Take Harkin for example, he's been under our eye for a long time."

"Who is he?" I said. "In my world he was just some pompous asshole from a rich family."

"He's pretty much the same in my world, but he's dangerous too. The Harkins are an old and powerful vampire family. Once upon a time they ruled everything. Over the years their innate strength naturally dwindled—"

"Why?"

"Inbreeding mostly. They wanted to keep the bloodlines pure, but it ended up making them weaker."

"Harkin is the product of inbreeding?"

Hunter smiled. "Kind of makes sense when you look at his face. They're not the strongest vampires anymore, but they still have a lot of money and influence. Harkin is desperate to get back on top, he can't stand the idea there are others out there that are more powerful than him."

"Having the amulet would tick that problem off."

"The amulet is powerful, and incredibly dangerous in the wrong hands, but there are lots of dangerous artifacts out there. Quite a few have gone missing recently, and we suspect Harkin's estate has something to do with it, though we haven't been able to prove it."

"You think he's hoarding these artifacts?"

"Most likely. The guardians have never found any evidence though. The working theory is that he's hoarding powerful items to help when the amulet is discovered again. Like now."

We had been walking through the house all the while, finally stopping in a grand master bedroom as our conversation came to a close. Hunter set our things down and stretched out his body.

"Where's your contact?" I asked.

"About a twenty-minute drive from here. His name is Juan and he runs a paranormal pawnshop, but it won't be open for a few more hours. We've got a little time to ourselves until then."

Hunter turned around to face me. Electricity crackled through the air.

"Oh," I said. "Have you got anything planned?"

He threaded his hands together, cracked his fingers and a dark smile crept over his face. "As it happens, I know a girl that's overdue a round of punishment or two." He took a step towards me and gently ran his hand down my face. I held my breath in anticipation, my body burning to feel his touch again.

"Really? It's hard to imagine a big strong man like you couldn't keep a small girl in check."

He smiled and kissed me, his tongue pushing against mine. Our mouths rolled together, locked in a long and deep embrace that left me floating.

"You'd be surprised," he said as he pulled away. "She's quite head-strong. Unlike anyone I've ever met before."

"Sounds like someone to keep hold of."

"Oh, I'm never letting go, if that's what she wants."

"She's definitely considering it."

The next second we were all over each other.

Our lips found one another again, coming together in a clash of passionate fury. My hands worked quickly, stripping him free of his cumbersome clothes until his flesh was pressed against mine.

In a matter of moments, I was down to my underwear and Hunter was too. He took me by the hand and led me over to the bed, my eyes unable to focus on anything else other than his hulking and muscular frame. He dwarfed me in every aspect, making me look like a doll in the hands of a minotaur.

He scooped me up off the floor and I wrapped my legs around his muscular waist, my pussy pressing up against his washboard abs. I held his face in my hands, kissing him deeply as he climbed onto the fourposter bed. He dropped forward and we crashed against the mattress, my body yielding into his as his weight surrounded me.

I could feel his huge cock burning against my dripping panties, his shaft digging forward as his hips tugged into mine.

"I want you..." I whispered in his ear, gasping as his lips moved over my neck. My fingers clawed against his broad and muscular back, pulling him closer, longing to be one.

A playful darkness glinted in his bright red eyes. He pulled back and pinned my arms above my head with one of his hands. "You have a lot to make up for, kitten," he growled.

"Show me," I pleaded, my breath trembling in anticipation.

Hunter pulled me up into a sitting position and used a belt to tie my arms behind my back. With one hand on my jaw he guided me into a crouching position on the floor by the bed. Then he inched forward and opened his legs. His mammoth erection pointed into the air.

"Good little slaves prove themselves," he said. "Show your master how much you care."

"Yes, sir," I whimpered, moving forward and opening my lips around the fat head of his bulbous cock. I took him in my mouth and inched forward, moving as far down his thick shaft as I could.

I couldn't quite make it all the way to the base, he was far too long for that, but I managed to get about halfway. Once I did, I looked up at him and saw him staring down at me. I drew my head back and started bobbing up and down his length, wiggling my tongue along the bottom of his shaft and picking up my pace.

Hunter slipped his fingers through my hair, applying pressure gently so his hands could follow my movement, not so much that he was moving me.

My hands were still bound behind my back, so I couldn't reach up and touch him, or myself, as much as I wanted to.

I pulled all the way back to his tip, letting my tongue kiss the end of his cock. For a moment I left him hanging there in the air, his cock throbbing with the want of my touch.

"You like this?" I said to him under lust-laden eyes. I could see his great barrel chest rising and falling quickly. His fingers pressed gently against my temples.

"Are you teasing me, slave?" he said.

I just shrugged my shoulders. "What are you going to do, punish me for it?"

Without waiting I thrust his cock back into my mouth, trying to go a little further this time, reaching for the thick base that eluded me. I'd never actually done anything like this with a man before, I guess my love life had always been a little vanilla before Hunter.

I was glad I was doing this with him though. He had a way of making me feel special and naughty, like I was the sexiest woman alive by teasing him in this way.

"God you're amazing..." he gasped above me. I could see his stomach start to tense. His legs trembled a little.

He was getting close.

"I love the taste of your cock, daddy," I teased.

If you'd told me I'd be talking dirty a week ago I would have called you a liar.

Hunter just had that effect on me.

The taste of sweet and salty precum came on my tongue, signaling that Hunter was close. I drew back and rolled my tongue slowly around his head, taking my movement to a deliberate crawl so to tease him one last time before release.

"Fuck..." he said, the word stretching over several aching syllables.

With that I pushed forward once more, taking his cock into my mouth as far as I possibly could. I felt his girth and length swell as his orgasm broke. I held my mouth around him, clamping my lips down as his cum exploded onto my tongue.

"Rachel!" he gasped, his hands now clasping down firmly on my head. He held me in place, his whole body shaking and his hot breath racing out in short and fiery bursts. I was so fucking turned on at the sound of his breath and the way he filled my mouth.

After several pumps he finally finished coming. I swallowed every drop down and pulled back, taking a huge breath of air as I looked up at Hunter. He dropped back to a lying position on the bed, his chest racing from his orgasm. I stood up and looked down at him.

"Did your little slave perform well?" I teased.

"Where the... how the... who the hell taught you that? That was amazing!"

"First time amigo," I said with a wink. "Maybe it was beginner's luck."

"Well you are *very* lucky," Hunter sat and pushed his weight back onto his elbows. His hungry eyes poured over my naked body. "I'll have a hard time following that."

"What does that mean?"

A shriek left my mouth as Hunter moved in a flash. Next thing I knew I was on my back with my legs in the air. My arms were now pinned underneath me, and the huge vampire was between my legs, his large hands pressed against the insides of my thighs. His face was mere inches from my pussy.

He leaned forward and pressed his lips against the damp fabric covering my sex. My panties were now soaked through for him. My entire body reacted to the touch, with bolts of lightning fizzing across my skin.

"Oh my god!" I said, stammering the words between choking breaths.

The huge vampire peeled my underwear away and threw them somewhere behind him. His lips came back, flesh touching flesh this time. The soft and warm rush of his breath sent chills up and down my spine. The deft cushion of his lips had my eyes rolling.

His thumbs squeezed into my thighs as he pushed his tongue against my wet folds. I opened around him, relaxing against his touch. He started at the very bottom of my slit, dragging his tongue up all the way to the bud, where his lips pursed around me and sucked ever so gently.

Heaven.

He repeated that action more times than I could count. With each repetition the sensations stacked on top of one another, my pleasure building with each moment until I couldn't take much more.

Breath juddering, stomach tensed, thighs knocking and body arching away from the mattress. I was only seconds away from finding my release and it felt fucking amazing.

That was when the vampire pulled away from me with a sharp movement, his red eyes waiting for me as I looked down.

"Hunter?" I said, panting the words through impatient disappointment.

He simply smiled. "What, did you think I was going to be that nice? You've been a bad girl, remember?"

"Please," I gasped. "I need this."

"And you'll get it little slave, all in due time."

The huge vampire wrapped his hand around my right leg and flipped me onto my front. Then he was behind me. He smoothed his hands over my ass and moved in close, letting his tongue probe my other hole.

"Fuck…" I gasped, unable to hide how good it felt. Was he going to torture every part of me?

"You're a naughty little slave, aren't you?" he said, the flat point of his tongue dancing around the tight ring. Looking over my shoulder I saw him sit up. He sliced his hand through the air, caning my already-delicate bottom with his palm.

I crowed his name as pain seared the flesh. The rush of heat was followed by a wave of pleasure that now felt all too familiar.

"You hit like a girl," I said, wanting him to go harder.

A dark laugh erupted from his chest. "Challenge accepted."

Hunter released the belt around my wrists and cracked it against my ass. This time I howled much louder. I gathered the bedding in my palms and balled my fists, cursing Hunter's name as fire erupted over my ass.

"Fucker!"

"I knew you'd like it," he said. I could practically hear him smiling.

I had to bite down on the blanket with the next couple of hits. Each one sounded louder than the last, numbing my flesh until I could only feel the rush of fire circling the tender area.

My poor little pussy was wet and trembling, aching to be taken by his huge cock. With each strike from his belt I was getting more turned on, and I knew he was too, how much longer could he last?

"You know, slave…" he said. "I was just thinking that myself."

It was easy to forget that my thoughts were no longer private around Hunter. I'd have to keep reminding myself of that fact if I ever wanted to win an argument against him. All of that left my mind though as Hunter threw the belt behind him and mounted me from behind.

He positioned me on the bed, moving me around like a living fuck doll. His hands forced my head down and he pulled my ass up.

The vampire gave me another little spank—for good measure—before grabbing hold of me and thrusting his cock deep inside my aching pussy. He speared deep, burying himself completely, and I let out a deep and satisfied groan that came from the very center of me.

The huge creature ravished me, his powerful and muscular body rolling into mine with a force that left the bed shaking. Long and deep thrusts mixed with hard and fast pumps that left me howling and breathless.

I cried his name over and over, my words now lost to a primal and guttural language of lust comprised only of the wildest sounds.

Time became a blur in his presence.

I came several times over, my tight walls squeezing around him and begging his cock for its sweet milk.

He came inside me, filling me with plumes of liquid fire that dribbled down my thighs. At some point we changed, and I was on top of him, rolling my hips and grinding up and down his long cock, which was still rock-solid despite him coming in me several times.

My hands explored his muscular body, appreciating his pecs, his chiseled abs, his muscular arms and powerful thighs. I moved in close and we kissed, losing ourselves in time as we forgot about everything else.

His strong arms wrapped around me and held me tight, his hips moving in time with my own as we approached a heedless crescendo. My cries of pleasure had shifted several octaves higher, my breath reserved now just for the sounds of appreciation I had for him.

It ended with one final explosion of fire.

Pleasure rippled through me like water, shattering through my body like a powerful tide through panes of glass. I clung onto him, pressed firm against his cock as we came together.

Every atom in my body sang with the heat of fire. We were planets colliding together, oceans of stars meeting in eternal darkness, galaxies spinning together to make something brilliant and beautiful, a new heaven comprised of two souls.

For the longest time we just lay like that, our sweaty bodies pressed against one another, melded together in the fires of lust. I could have slept like that I was so comfortable. His body was the missing jigsaw piece against my own.

We did part eventually. I think we might have even drifted off for a few minutes. It felt so right in his presence it was easy to forget about the impending apocalypse.

Life always had a way of catching up to you though. It came in the form of Hunter's phone ringing.

"I should probably get that," he said with a regretful sigh, "Given the current state of things."

I watched the naked giant as he padded across the room and pulled his phone from his jacket. He put it on speaker and set it down on a bedside table while he sat down and brushed his hand up my side.

"Hello?"

"Hunter, it's Rocky. Did you get out okay?"

"We did," he said. "How are things there?"

"They've been better. My EMP managed to take care of Harkin's mech-suit plan, but he had other aces up his sleeve. Turns out he had a demon stone."

"Fuck."

"Yeah."

"What's a demon stone?" I asked.

"Oh, hey Rachel," Rocky said. "A demon stone is a rare artifact, an opal imbued with the magic of a powerful being. They can be used to fortify armies, giving one man the strength of ten. It's turned Harkin's goons into a group of super-vampires."

"Stronger than guardians?" I asked.

"It's hard to tell. I'd say the playing field is much more level now," Rocky said. "The attack on HQ was bad, really bad. Chase and his unit fucked us over big time, but I'm not even at the worst part yet."

"Oh good," Hunter said. "What else?"

"They got Saydra. They kidnapped her. I imagine she'll try to go as long as she can without cooperating, but who knows what else Harkin has up his sleeve. It won't be long before she gives into his torture. And when that happens…"

"Yeah I know," Hunter said. "She'll lead him straight to us."

"Hunter do you need backup? When Harkin and his men catch up to you, you won't stand a chance."

"No," Hunter looked at me and shook his head. "Not yet, anyway. Saydra said our chances are best on our own. I'll call if and when that changes. We'll just have to get a move on."

"Are you any closer?"

"We're in the right place, we just need to find the person we're looking for. I'd be more specific, but—"

"Don't be," Rocky interrupted. "I've taken every care to make sure this channel is secure, but there's no telling how safe it is now. Just call if you need anything, and good luck, okay?"

Hunter laughed. "We don't need luck. We've got Doctor Stone on our side."

He ended the call and sighed.

"Looks like things are getting worse out there," I said.

"Harkin is starting to move his pieces into place. His goons can fight off the guardians now *and* he has Saydra. I don't like how this is going."

"We need to find Nalinth and talk with her before Harkin traces us here," I said.

He nodded. "Yeah, we need to get a move on. Let's clean up and get dressed. I'll have to make Juan open shop early. I just hope to god he can tell us where the dark witch is."

Hunter got up from the bed and made his way to the en suite to shower. I followed him, allowing myself one more moment of relaxation as I joined him in the steaming water.

I couldn't help noticing the sinking feeling at the pit of my stomach though.

Harkin was closing in.

Was he going to win?

12

HUNTER

*R*achel and I were out the door shortly after Rocky's call. Juan Ferrero was an informant of mine who had helped me out several times in the past. He was a criminal, and his paranormal pawnshop regularly fenced powerful stolen artifacts, but he was also a magnet for gossip and extremely valuable for street-level gossip.

I pulled the Bugatti up on the sidewalk and we got out. Juan's shop was in a less-than-desirable part of the town. The car was kitted with some interesting alarm systems though, and any thieves or vandals would be in for a surprise if they put a finger out of line.

The shop was still locked up. Juan kept odd hours and didn't open doors until six in the evening. We were an hour early, but I knew he'd be up.

With one well-placed boot I broke open the locked front doors and walked into the shop with my shotgun pointed right at Juan. He was sitting at the counter, thumbing through a magazine. Juan threw both his hands in the air and jumped to his feet.

"Hey, hey! Holy shit! Easy now! Hunter?! What's going on here?!"

Juan looked human, in a way. He was tall, gaunt, pale and always looked ill. The truth was that he was a Nemademon, a small parasitic entity taking up residence in a fresh corpse. It wasn't against the law, as long as the Nemademon had a permit and followed a long list of specific rules.

"I need information and I need it fast," I said.

"I don't know!" Juan said. I fired the shotgun up into the ceiling and plastered him with dust. "Hey, what the fuck?! I said I don't know!"

"You don't even know what I'm after," I growled, pumping the shotgun to fire again. "The next round will go straight into your head. You don't want to lose this body, do you?"

"Will you talk some sense into him?!" Juan pleaded to Rachel. "He's going to kill me!"

"Uhm…" Rachel said to me. "Perhaps murder is a little excessive. We can't get answers out of him, if he's dead."

"He's a Nemademon," I said to her. "A small parasitic demon living in a dead body. He's actually very hard to kill, believe it or not."

I fired again, covering Juan with more dust.

"Shit!" he screamed. "Stop! What do you want to know?!"

"Any new churches around here?" I asked.

Juan laughed; his hands were still in the air. "You'll have to be more specific than that, Hunter, this is Louisiana. Churches open and close all the time."

"A voodoo church," Rachel interjected. "On a lake. Probably being run by a priestess."

Juan's eyes darted about in his skull before he answered. "I ain't heard anything about no church like that."

I fired again, covering him with more dust.

"Fuck!" he screamed. "Stop fucking shooting up my store!"

"The next round will be in your head, and then your body is ruined. I'm willing to bet a stupid Nemademon like you doesn't have body insurance."

"I just forgot to set up the renewal, that's all!"

I pumped the gun. "Last chance."

"Okay, okay! Just chill! I might have heard about something like that." He looked at Rachel. "I'll talk to you, you're reasonable."

"What do you know?" she asked.

"I heard there's some new voodoo church up in Coushatta, but that's all I know."

"In your head," I reminded him.

"Okay! It's big business! The whole town's going every Sunday! The church is only new, but it's got a huge congregation. Word has it some priestess is in charge..."

Rachel and I looked at one another. "Nalinth."

"So, are we done here?" Juan laughed nervously. "Well if that's all you need—"

I saw the flash of his handgun as he reached for it. A second later my shotgun discharged, and Juan's body was blown across the wall behind the counter. The body slumped to the floor, the face burst open and a shiny black figure jumped onto the glass countertop.

"You prick!" Juan shouted; his voice much higher now he was in his Nemademon form. Nemademons were humanoid, but they were about the size of a pint glass. They had an obsidian exoskeleton, which made them very hard to kill. "Do you know how much a replacement body is going to cost me?! I'm supposed to open in an hour!"

"You were reaching for your gun," I said.

"You've been shooting at me!"

"Is there something you're not telling me about this church? My bullets might not be able to kill you, but I *do* know the one way to kill a Nemademon."

The tiny little figurine suddenly backed up on the counter. "Shit, all right, just leave me alone, Hunter. Fuck man. The priestess running this church is serious business. She's got hooks in everything. Several of her followers have come through this shop, they creep me the fuck out."

"You know anything else?"

"Yeah, things have been heating up since that volcano erupted. Mambo says it's the end of times. Rumor has it they're straight up sacrificing people up there."

"Wouldn't the police stop something like that?" Rachel asked.

Juan laughed. "She's got her hooks in *everything*, lady. This woman, she has a weird hypnotic power."

"Have you met her?" I asked.

"Fuck have I," Juan said. "I'm not going anywhere near that."

"What's her name?" Rachel asked.

"They just call her Mambo."

I turned to look at Rachel. "We've got everything we need, let's go."

We turned to leave. As we did Juan called after me. "Hunter, I'm warning you man, be careful around this woman. She's the real deal!"

I was already aware of that. I'd dealt with Nalinth once before. The last time we met she warned me what would happen. I just hoped she was wrong.

I'd only just found my mate.

I wasn't ready to die just yet.

"Why am I beyond creeped out right now?" Rachel asked as we drove through the town.

It looked like the rest of the world was getting on with things despite the ever dark, but as soon as we entered the boundaries of Coushatta, I was hit with the distinct impression that something was *very* wrong.

"Empty streets, empty buildings... something's not right." We hadn't actually stopped in any buildings to see if they were empty. All the doors and windows had been left open however, like the entire town had decided to collectively air out their property.

The other strange thing was how *still* everything felt. I had the car almost at a crawl now, driving down streets at just above a jogging pace because I was creeped out too. The leaves in the trees were completely still, if there was a breeze or a sound then I didn't hear one, not even with my advanced vampire senses.

I pulled up in the abandoned town square and got out of the car. That was another reason the town looked so weird.

Where had all the cars gone?

Rachel stepped onto the sidewalk and we looked at one another, letting the silence talk for us.

The hairs were standing on the back of my neck.

"I don't like this," she said in a quiet voice.

"That makes two of us," I whispered back.

There was a discernable electricity in the air that just couldn't be ignored, a prickly feeling that made my stomach run cold and made me want to look over my shoulder.

Nalinth was here, of that I was sure, but what was she up to?

"Hunter!" Rachel hissed. "Did you hear that?"

Rachel's gaze shot to the west. There a row of buildings backed onto parkland. A long flat hill slowly led down a dark body of murky water, where a jungle of twisting cypress trees stretched into the night. There was nothing but silence.

"Rachel, I have super hearing, and I didn't hear a damned thing."

"It was a drum," she said, starting in the direction of the supposed sound. "Look, there it is again, louder! Let's go!"

Rachel broke into a brisk walk, leaving the street behind and heading onto the grass that led down to the bayou proper. I followed her, staying close behind. Every fifteen seconds or so she would remark about the strange drumming sound, the one that I, for some reason, could not hear.

"It's deafening now!" she shouted over the silence. "Can't you hear it?!" She had her hands over her ears. The only sound was her voice, which echoed through the trees.

At the bottom of the hill a wooden bridge arched over the water. As we rounded a natural corner of trees, I saw more bridges linking smaller islands together. There were lights in the distance now. Rachel immediately stepped onto the bridge.

I followed her.

In a minute or so we were almost completely across the large body of water, and as we came around another natural corner the lake properly came into view. We both came to a stop at seeing the large black wooden cathedral looming high above us.

"What in the ever-loving fuck…" I whispered.

A hundred lanterns illuminated the dark building and its eerie gothic spires. In the lake surrounding the island there had to be a thousand small boats, all with lanterns too, waiting in the water, all packed together, looking like rays coming from a sun.

There were people everywhere.

Standing in boats, standing on the island and looking up at the church. They were all statues, eerily silent, their attention fixed on a balcony halfway up the church's front. A woman was standing there.

Her eyes were whiter than bone. The untamable black hair on her head reminded me of a snake nest. She wore a long black dress with blood red flowers upon it. Intricate cords of bone jewelry hung loose around her throat. Empty white eyes were glaring right at us, whiter only than the teeth shining in her impossibly wide grin.

Nalinth.

On the balcony behind her a topless man beat his arm against a giant drum. The drum made no sound when it played, but Rachel seemed to hear it.

"Hunter," Nalinth said, her voice cutting across the still darkness like a knife. "I warned you what would happen if you came back here. You will die at my hand."

"I assume you know why we're here," I shouted back to her. I couldn't get over how *quiet* things were. There wasn't a leaf out of place, or even the choral chirp of the cicadas. Just deathly silence, and glassy black water.

The dark witch nodded. "You have the amulet again," she said, her white eyes now boring into Rachel. "Will you kill this keeper too?"

"Please," Rachel said, interrupting the witch. "We need your help. Can you tell me how to use the amulet? If we don't find the tomb in time, the sun won't come back out again."

Nalinth laughed slowly. It was a twisted sound, unearthly and unnatural, it sent more chills down my spine.

"Did Hunter explain who I am?" Nalinth said to Rachel. "Why he won't kill me, even though he so easily could?"

Rachel looked at me and back at Nalinth. "No?"

"She's a necromancer," I explained to Rachel. "Her power comes from obtaining followers. Once they are in her thrall, she can command them to do whatever she likes. All these people are under her control."

"You missed out the best part, Hunter," she said, looking at Rachel. "If I die, then they all die. You see, I know Hunter can never condemn a group of innocents to death like that, so he can do nothing to stop me."

"Normally you'd be right, Nalinth," I said. "But if I don't get the answers we need then the whole planet dies. The numbers alone make sense."

"You helped last time," Rachel pleaded. "Why not help again?"

"I was weak last time," Nalinth said. "This time I am not. I will take the amulet for myself and give myself the ultimate power that I so rightly deserve. I give you a choice now. Give me the amulet or I will take it."

"You're not the keeper," I said to the dark witch. "It's not meant for you."

Nalinth cackled. "Don't waste my time, Hunter. We both know I'm strong enough to handle this. Now... hand it over, or you both die."

"I know there's still good inside of you," I said to the dark witch. "See reason here. Don't let this dark magic control you. Think of Davian. What would he think to see you like this?"

"Don't you dare mention his name here!" Nalinth roared, her face contorting in an expression of demonic fury. As she did her followers all turned to face us.

"Ah, fuck," I whispered.

"You have wasted too much time now!" she said. "No longer! Seize them. Kill them both and get the—"

Nalinth paused as Rachel dropped to the ground. She was breathing loudly, her hands stretched out on the dirt. "Legba!" Rachel shouted. "Legba! Legba!"

"Rachel?" I said, moving forward to help her.

"Stop!" Rachel shouted. "He has me! Legba has me! He commands me! He says to go to her! To Nalinth! To Mambo! The black witch must have the amulet!"

For a moment Nalinth and I were joined in our mutual confusion. Rachel looked at me from the side of her eye, and I heard the faintest whisper of suggestion in my mind.

Trust me.

"Papa Legba," Nalinth gasped. "He has taken control of her. Come to me at once, girl! Bring the amulet. Your goddess wills it!"

Rachel dropped to the ground and rolled onto her back. She clawed at the air and gasped for breath, acting like she was possessed by a powerful voodoo spirit. I had to give it to her, the display was impressive. If the whole historian thing hadn't worked out, she could have been a convincing actor.

"Take me to her!" she said in a deep and gravelly voice. She pointed at me, curling her fingers like her hands were plagued with arthritis. I scooped her up from the ground and whispered in her ear.

"This better be a damned good plan."

"To the priestess!" she shouted. "Legba commands it!"

I held Rachel in my arms and walked across the final bridge to the main island. Nalinth's army of thralls all stared back at me, their white eyes glistening in the torchlight. I'd seen some unnerving things in my time, but this was definitely up there.

Silence smothered me like a lead cloak.

As I stepped onto the island the crowds all parted at once, stepping aside to make a clear path towards the church. I really didn't want to step inside the church, every instinct in my body was telling me not to.

Thankfully I didn't have to. Nalinth had come downstairs and met us just as we got to the front door. Physically she wasn't a threat at all, but with the snap of her fingers she could have her followers tear me to shreds. I might have been a guardian, but even I didn't fancy my chances against a thousand possessed humans.

"Put her down and stay back," Nalinth said. I prayed to myself that Rachel had a plan here. Nalinth was *not* someone to mess around with. I set Rachel down on the dirt outside the front door and she held the amulet up in one hand.

"For you, Priestess Mambo!" Rachel said. She had rolled her eyes back in her head for effect. "Legba commands me to give it to you!"

Nalinth smiled, her white eyes glinting with the promise of great and terrible power. If I moved quickly enough, I could snatch the amulet out of Rachel's hand, grab her off the floor and get out of here before things got really bad.

No. I had to trust Rachel. Her brain had got us out of trouble once before. It was time I started listening to her.

Nalinth reached her hand out slowly and took the amulet from Rachel. I felt my stomach drop then. Giving an artifact so powerful to a dark creature like Nalinth was basically game over. I hoped Rachel had something good.

"Finally," Nalinth said, her voice breaking with excitement. "It is mine. Do you realize how long I've waited? What I had to do to get this? The years I've waited?"

"You could have easily taken it off us last time," I said to her. "Nothing stopped you then."

"Oh, but it did," the dark witch said. "I consulted the threads of time. Taking the amulet for myself then, it never would have worked. That's why I had to poison your friend's mind. I infected his soul with my dark energy and had him kill his mate. If I could wait, and see the amulet again, it would be mine, and here we are..."

I felt my world shattering in two.

"Wait. You're the one that warped Trey. Not the amulet?"

Nalinth just cackled. "A small price to pay for victory," she said. "And now you will die too, Hunter. The voice of Legba has blessed your mate's ear. She is in my control now, you have—"

"Actually," Rachel said, sitting up from the floor, "I didn't hear the voice of Papa Legba. I just made all that stuff up."

Nalinth froze. "You, you what?!"

"Yeah, you see, I did a term on religious iconography, and I learned quite a lot about voodoo during that time. I figured if I threw out some basic terminology, I could gain your trust and get close."

"But I have the amulet, you stupid bitch!" Nalinth laughed to herself. "I got exactly what I wanted!"

"And… so did I. Or Halo at least. Yeah, you see, I've been hearing her voice ever since I got the amulet, and she told me to give it to you. So, here we are. She hasn't steered me wrong so far. I'm guessing there had to be a pretty good reason."

And then I saw what the reason was.

The chain from the amulet had wrapped itself around Nalinth's wrist like a snake. The stone started glowing, until the light shining from it was brighter than a blinding star.

"Stop!" Nalinth shouted. "Stop it! Take it back! I don't want it! It burns!"

I grabbed Rachel and sprinted away from the island, just as the explosion of divine light ripped through the church behind us. This blast seemed far bigger than the one in the restaurant, and probably with good reason. Nalinth was stronger than a pack of vampire bikers, Halo probably had more strength set aside to deal with her.

A shockwave burst across the clearing, knocking back every thrall standing around the church. It carried on across the dark water as a wave which made boats rock and knock together. When it finally hit the far banks, I noticed the leaves were moving in the trees again. The sounds of the swamp had returned.

The silence was gone.

One by one we saw the thralls standing up. They looked a little confused, but the congregation made their way back over the bridge, passing Rachel and I without even looking our way.

"Where are they going?" Rachel asked. Even the boats were leaving now.

"It looks like the blast broke Nalinth's hold over them. Hopefully they go back to their beds and forget all about this."

When the last of the flock had left the island Rachel and I went back over the bridge. Nalinth was lying in the doorway to her church, the amulet on the dirt beside her. She saw us approaching and blinked slowly.

"I couldn't contain the power."

"I tried to warn you," I said. "The amulet is for the keeper only."

"You are the one," she said to Rachel. "I see that now. I will help you."

Rachel crouched down and gathered the amulet off the ground. "Thank you. How do we find Halo?"

"Do you know what an anthelion is?" Nalinth said, her voice barely higher than a whisper.

Rachel nodded. "An optical illusion. It looks like there are three suns in the sky."

"Correct. Like the anthelion, you need to use the amulet three times to find the tomb. You have already used it twice."

"I have?" Rachel asked.

"Yes," Nalinth said. "A flare in the restaurant, I can see. And a flare now. You have created two points of light. You need one more and you can triangulate the tomb's location. The third point will be equidistant to the others, to create a perfect triangle."

Rachel looked perplexed. "What does that mean?"

Nalinth's eyes rolled back in her skull. "You made a point in New York. The second was here in Louisiana, 1,500 miles away. The third should be 1,500 miles away from both of those, which will make a perfect triangle."

I tried to do the mental geography in my head. "Wait a second, that would put the third point somewhere in Minnesota."

"Minnesota?" Rachel said. "What's in Minnesota?"

That's when it hit me. I knew exactly what was there. "The headquarters for Harkin corporation. The amulet…"

"It's taking us straight to him!" Rachel said.

"Hunter," Nalinth wheezed. "My sister warned you that one of us would have to die for you to leave here. I thought it would be you, but I was wrong. It was me, Hunter. I am the one that must die. Tell her I am sorry and tell Davian… tell him that I am sorry too."

"He knows," I said. They were the only words I could offer before the dark witch closed her eyes one last time. As she did Rachel stood up. We stepped back and watched as the witch's body disappeared on the wind.

"You heard her," Rachel said. "One more point and then we can find the tomb."

"All we have to do is fly straight into the jaws of death," I said.

"We need backup now," Rachel said. "Hunter, we can't take Harkin on alone without the rest of the guardians. Fighting together is the only way we'll survive."

She was right.

Or mostly right anyway.

The amulet was sending us right into the belly of the beast. Harkin HQ was a fortress in its own right, there was no telling what kind of traps lay in wait for us there.

Going there of our own volition was almost certainly a death sentence.

Even with the guardians behind us.

13

RACHEL

*I*t wasn't long before we were leaving the dark skies of Louisiana far behind us. Hunter and I had quickly made our way back to the landing strip and were back in the sky once more, heading towards… Minnesota.

The amulet was sending us straight into the arms of Harkin, our most dangerous enemy.

"None of this makes any sense," I said to Hunter, who had his hands on the joysticks and his eyes on the clouds in front of us. I remember he said the search was different every time. "Is this what the search involved last time? Did you have to use three points then?"

"It was quite different last time," Hunter said to me. "Even the amulet was different, it didn't look like it does now."

"Different? What do you mean? What was different about it?"

"Well it was still an amulet," Hunter said, glancing across the cockpit as I pulled the amulet out and unwrapped it. "It had a stone in the middle, but it also had a dial around the outside. The dial moved depending on our orientation, and as we followed it the stone would start blinking more frequently. It was basically a giant game of hot and cold."

"Huh. What did it lead to?"

"It took us all over. We went to Cairo, Shanghai, Morocco... the damned thing had us running all over the planet. It was leading us to scattered pieces of an ancient necklace. There were nine fragments in all, and the last one was in Ireland, right where Halo's hiding place was. When we combined the pieces, the tomb revealed itself."

"Did this necklace have four main stones, each with lots of little stones around it?"

Hunter's face lit up. "Yeah! Do you know it?"

"That's the necklace of seasons, Halo is always depicted wearing it. Each stone represents a season of the year, and the smaller stones around it represents the days in those seasons. What happened to it?"

"Halo took it and thanked us for returning the necklace when we got to the tomb, and then Trey..." Hunter paused momentarily. "That's when he flipped and attacked Laurelai."

"What happened after that?" I said, keen to not make Hunter dwell too long on the dark parts.

"I pretty much had to use the wish. Halo said the search wouldn't be the same the next time. She said it changes every time, to stop people from abusing the search."

"So, everything we're doing now, is completely different."

"Almost," Hunter said.

"Almost?"

"Yeah, well, this part is similar to the end of the last hunt. There was an anthelion then too. Three points made a perfect triangle, and at the center of that triangle was the location leading to the tomb. That point was at the most southern part of New Zealand."

"Wait, what? How did that lead you to Ireland?"

"Antipodes," Hunter said.

I blinked. "What?"

Hunter grinned. "Have I finally found something you don't know?"

My brow furrowed as I slowly tried to figure the word out. "If you were to drill a hole right through the earth from New Zealand..."

"You'd end up in Southern Ireland. Correct. I guess you do know it all," he said with a smile.

"So, we're forming a triangle now to find its center," I recapped.

"Yeah."

"And the triangle's center will be on the exact opposite side of the globe to Halo's new hiding spot."

"Yeah, and?"

"And? So why don't we just figure it out manually instead of going to Harkin's HQ?!" I shouted. "Do you have a map in here somewhere?"

Hunter's mouth dropped open as he caught up. "The compartment on the dashboard in front of you, there's a tablet with some digital mapping software!" I pulled the tablet out, unlocked the screen and a second later I had a digital map of the united states under my fingers. "There are tools to put down points and lines—" Hunter began to explain.

"I've figured that out already!" I said. "Let me work in peace!"

I began throwing down points and lines on the map, making a triangle from the three anthelion points. One in New York, one in Louisiana, and one... somewhere in northwest Minnesota. As I was working a call came in from Rocky.

Hunter took it.

"Please tell me you have some good news?" Hunter said to Rocky.

"Just checking in on my favorite treasure hunters. Couldn't help noticing that we have two days left and err... you guys haven't given us any updates." He laughed nervously. "Hopefully we're closer to the truth?"

"Cut it with the fucking manners!" an abrupt voice cut in. I instantly looked up from my work and saw Commander Davian had burst on to the screen. He snatched the camera from Rocky's hands. "Well if it isn't princess fucking Hunter and his four-eyes girlfriend."

"Good to see he survived the attack on HQ..." I mumbled to myself. Hunter glanced over at me and smiled.

"Oh Commander, so good to see you're alive."

"We're all alive dipshit!" Davian barked. He swung the tablet around and revealed a room full of guardians. Hunter's entire unit was there. "HQ is fucking destroyed, and we've gone into hiding. Now give me some good fucking news!"

"The amulet is leading us straight to Harkin," Hunter said. "But

Rachel thinks she can cut out a few steps and find the tomb." He looked at me. "Right, Rachel?"

I looked up from my notes and saw a screen full of expectant faces staring at me. "Is that right?" Davian said. "What are you doing?"

"Some basic trigonometry and mapping," I said. "Now if you'll let me concentrate—"

"Assist her Rocky! I need to scream at Hunter!" Davian shouted. A second later another screen on the cockpit lit up and I saw Rocky's face.

"I've split the call," Rocky explained. Davian was still shouting into the screen facing Hunter, who had quickly hit mute to silence his commander. "What are you working on? Do you need help?"

I very quickly explained the anthelion triangle to Rocky, and how it's central point could inadvertently lead to Halo's new resting place. "I get it!" he shouted eagerly about halfway through my explanation. "Let me run it through some mapping software and we can calculate it precisely to a few feet. I can have you an answer in—"

Rocky froze then, prompting me and Hunter to look up at the screen. Rocky's attention was slightly off camera. I noticed that Davian's muted image had paused too.

"Hey," Hunter said loudly. "Why have you both stopped?"

"Hunter it's your airspace," Rocky said in a warning tone. He instantly dropped what he was doing and wheeled over to another terminal, taking his tablet with him. "You're in the Xexos-4, right? The same one I had stashed on the back dock?"

"Yeah, why, what's up?"

"Well I'm tracing your position on the radar, it looks like you're flying north-west, presumably to find this last point in Minnesota."

"That's us, data confirmed," Hunter said. "Now tell me what you can see that has you sweating so badly."

"Your onboard radar only stretches so far. The radar I have here extends three times that distance. You've got company heading your way, directly from the front, it looks like a whole group of jets."

"Jesus Christ..." Hunter said to himself.

"Harkin," I said in realization.

"It has to be," Rocky said. "He must have got your location from Saydra. She must have finally cracked under his interrogation. He's using her psychic powers against her."

The image quickly snapped away from Rocky as Davian stole the tablet once more. "Oh, very fucking funny, putting your commander on mute, you prick! Now you listen to me and listen carefully, you haven't got time to run away from this Hunter, you'll have to fight!"

As he said the words the blips came onto our local radar. It showed ten points moving towards us at a very fast speed.

"What a lovely welcome party," Hunter muttered. "Ten jets. Commander, I'm not fucking Briggs, I can't win in a dogfight against ten jets."

Just then another guardian pushed onto the frame. He was another giant man, but with short and curly chestnut hair. "You're not Briggs, but I am," he said to Hunter. "Are you listening carefully?"

"All ears," Hunter said.

"You don't have to win," Briggs said, "You just have to survive. If you unload all your missiles now and launch flares it will distract them so you can dive to the ground and find a safe landing spot."

"I like the first part," Hunter said.

He started flipping switches and hitting buttons.

As he did missiles screamed from the front of the jet, tearing through the night sky in front of us. I counted twelve from each side. They streamed into the distance and I saw the points on the radar scatter. Next up was the flare. After Hunter deployed that he pushed the joystick forward and we started to descend rapidly.

"Brilliant!" Briggs said. "Textbook, now you just need to—"

The image cut out and was replaced with one of Harkin.

"Hello!" he said cheerily. "It's come to my attention that you're not willing to cooperate."

"Go fuck yourself Harkin," Hunter growled.

"Did you know I have your psychic, Hunter?" Harkin replied. He turned the camera around and revealed a woman bound to a chair. "She's been quite helpful, very helpful in fact. She knows how this whole thing ends, and all I need now is that amulet. You and the girl? No longer necessary!"

As he said the words an alarm started flashing in the cockpit. "Warning! Projectile incoming!"

"Shit!" Hunter said, throwing the jet into a tight spiral to dodge the missile. It zoomed right over the cockpit window, missing us by inches. "Are you crazy?!" he shouted at Harkin. "If you blow us out of the sky, and we all lose!"

"Oh, I'm sure the amulet will be fine," Harkin laughed. "And I have my psychic witch to help find it. The pieces of your blown-up bodies... they don't matter. Now if you want to escape with your lives—"

"Sorry Harkin," Hunter shouted over the cockpit. "I've got another call on the line, but don't forget to go and fuck yourself!" He terminated the call and the guardians came back up on screen.

"Hunter?!" Davian shouted. "We're scrambling backup now; we'll be there as fast as we can!"

"Not fast enough!" Hunter shouted. "Rachel, hold on!" He pushed the stick further. We broke through the cloud and saw the lights of the world below us. The surface was fast approaching. I gripped the arms of my seat, wind roaring all around the straining cockpit.

"Warning, warning! Several projectiles incoming!"

Flashing red lights, the wail of wind, the judder of the jet, and the threat of imminent death. Hunter whirled the jet through a string of missiles, but our luck could only go so far. The first blast caught the right wing, sending us into an out of control spiral that left me reeling.

I was suddenly aware of Hunter. He was up from his chair and fastening something around me. "What are you doing?!" I shouted over the jet's drone, trying hard not to pass out from the g-force.

"Parachute! We have to eject! We're going down! Are you ready?!"

I tried my best to nod back at him. He equipped a parachute for himself and sat back in the chair. "We have to eject from the seats, but we'll go at the same time. I'll find you in the air, I've done this a hundred times before!"

He squeezed my hand one last time and he pressed a red button at the console's center. Nothing happened.

He pressed again.

Nothing.

"Hunter?!" I shouted.

"The eject system!" he said. "It's damaged from the hit. There's only enough gas to eject one seat!"

I already knew what was coming next. He did it before I could even stop him. Hunter flipped a switch and hit the button again. The world went into momentary slow motion as my seat launched up and out of the craft. I screamed, not for fear of what would happen next, but because Hunter was trapped in the jet.

The deafening rush of wind filled my ears. My seat span at all angles before my straps fell away, letting the seat fall to the earth below. Then my chute activated. The force took my breath away as my speed abruptly changed. I was no longer falling to my death; I was soaring down to the ground.

I had no idea how high up I was, but I estimated I had a few minutes of soaring until I would touch down. The sound of jets roared in the air overhead. Things were surprisingly quiet, until I saw our own jet spiral down.

"Hunter!" I screamed.

The plane hit the earth about a mile to my right, coming down in thick forest and illuminating the night with a bright ball of fire. I felt my heart twisting in my throat. Tears started down my face. I couldn't breathe.

Was Hunter... was Hunter dead?

I came down in thick forest. Steering the parachute was too difficult. I got caught in a tall pine, ended up wrapping around the thing and getting the shit beaten out of me by branches on the way down.

The chute's strings kept me from smashing against the ground like an egg, but they left me dangling a few feet above it, bruised and battered from my crash landing. I was in a dark forest, stranded in the middle of nowhere, sobbing to myself at having just seen my mate die an almost certain death.

My head hurt like a bitch, and my temples throbbed from my chaotic landing. Eyes growing heavy, I lost consciousness for a short while until I heard voices shouting in the distance.

"Up here!" they said. "The witch says it's this way!"

My heart dropped to my stomach as I saw light in the trees. Long shadows twisted across the ground. Red eyes flashed in the darkness. Flashlights finally caught me. I had no energy left to fight or run.

"There! Up there!"

The men were practically laughing when they finally reached me. I couldn't run even if I wanted to. I was dangling upside down, at head height with them.

"Ah, Doctor Stone," the vampire said. He was clearly one of Harkin's goons. "Mr. Harkin will be delighted to hear that you survived the attack. We're here to escort the amulet back to him, but as you're alive, we'll be taking you too. Sorry about your friend. He didn't survive the crash."

"Go and fuck yourself," I hissed at the goon.

The men just laughed amongst themselves. "I think this will be a lot easier for all of us without your smart mouth, don't you?"

He swung his elbow through the air and connected it with my face.

Everything turned to darkness.

14

HUNTER

I chose Rachel as soon as I knew the eject systems were damaged. With one switch I could re-route the remaining gas cylinders to her chair, meaning she would be able to escape alive. As soon as I hit the button her chair launched out of the jet, and I knew that she was safe.

That just left me trapped in a jet that was going to smash into the ground in the next twelve seconds.

With the ejector seat not working there was no point in staying in the chair. I had a chute and all I had to do was jump out manually. Easier said than done when the jet was spinning around two times a second.

I unbuckled myself, wrapped my hands around the cockpit—which now had no window—and pulled myself up. The wind was ferocious, and the jet's rapid spinning was both disorientating and nauseating. I was about to pull myself out when I heard the jet's AI blast another warning into the night.

"Inbound projectile, warning, warning!"

I saw the thing heading right for me. One last missile to blow the jet sky high and send me to hell. With one last kick I jumped from the ship just as the missile hit. I was caught up in the resulting fireball for a few seconds before the jet and I separated very quickly. I was spinning through the night, falling towards the ground as I tried to fan out any wayward flames on my body.

The fire went out pretty quickly thanks to me falling through the air, but I'd underestimated the damage the explosion had done when I pulled the cord for my chute. The bag opened and the chute went up, but as soon as I felt myself slow down, I knew that something was wrong, I was still going far too fast.

When I looked up, I realized that half of the chute had been burned up in the explosion, there were parts of it still on fire now. Two of the four strings tying me to the chute snapped simultaneously and then I was falling again, twisting through the air with a hunk of burning cloth chasing after me.

Something exploded in the distance, probably the jet Rachel and I had just tumbled out of. I was falling—nearly at full speed, but not quite—with the ground rushing towards me at 60 meters per second. I had about fifteen seconds before I would hit the floor and become a vampire puree. I had to think.

Fast.

My training had prepared me for an event like this, but the added bonus of being tied up in a burning parachute had never been factored in. It meant this real problem was much harder.

There were ways to hit the ground and survive a fall from an airplane—believe it or not—but that was the *last* option, and currently my only option.

I guess that was my plan then.

I scanned the approaching ground as quickly as I could. There was forest, a lake, fields of wheat and a river winding through a rocky gorge. The forest was probably my best bet. It would hurt like hell, but the branches could slow me down enough that by the time I hit the ground I might be going slow enough to survive.

Maybe.

But then I noticed something else, my bright red eyes glanced a silhouette in the darkness. The outline of a barn. That could be perfect. The fall would kill a human, probably even a vampire, but a guardian like myself?

I might only die a horrible death.

With one arm free I clutched the tattered controls and steered my fall towards the barn roof. I just about managed to line myself up with the roof. When I was five seconds out I screwed my body up into a ball and—

I smashed through the roof like a boulder through glass.

Roof tiles and wooden beams shattered around my hulking frame as I crashed down towards earth. My burning chute was torn from my body as I plummeted through rafters.

I never thought a barn would kick the absolute shit out of me, but I bounced through a tangle of wooden columns, thoroughly battered as I crunched through the floor of the loft section.

I finally got a happy ending when I felt myself collapsing through a tall tower of something soft and dry. I was finally still, motionless and lying on my back, looking up through the holes that my body had blown through the roof and loft above me.

Looking around I saw tall piles of hay on all sides. I had thundered right through the top of a haystack and tore right to its bottom. It felt like more than one bone was broken. Every breath was agony and I didn't even want to think about sitting up.

But I was alive.

The ground felt warm and wet beneath me. I was bleeding. Just a question of how much.

I managed to lift my head and looked down at my torso. There was quite a lot of blood.

Not ideal.

With no other choice I wrapped my hand around my right wrist and pressed the button on the subdermal chip buried just below the surface of my skin. I had just activated the emergency beacon, telegraphing my location to my guardian unit.

Eyes drifting, I started to wonder if Rachel was okay, and how many minutes I had before I was going to die.

Hopefully the guardians could get to me before then.

"Found the ugly son of a bitch, he's in a bad way. Let's get a drip on him immediately. Striker, can you suture these wounds? They don't need to look pretty."

I drifted in and out of consciousness, fading between unknown realms of black and a blurred and confusing reality. Bright lights blurred in my vision. Sounds echoed on all sides. I heard Davian shouting profanity-laden commands as I tried to keep my eyes open.

"Ash!" Davian shouted. "Go talk to Briggs, see how far out we are!"

Darkness.

"Striker! Is he going to live or not? We need this son of a bitch alive!"

Nothing.

"Rocky if this intel isn't good I swear to god I'll—!"

Black.

The next time I opened my eyes things were quieter. I saw Striker, the lone wolf of our unit. I was lying in a medical bed and he was standing over me, looking at charts and monitoring flashing screens besides me.

"Rachel," I said.

"She's alive. You on the other hand. Not so close."

"Where is she?"

"Harkin's men got her. We're on the way to get her back now."

Rage consumed me. I moved to sit up, but every small movement was agonizing pain.

"Easy now," Striker said. "You're in a bad way."

"How bad is it?" I wheezed.

"You're still one ugly son of a bitch," he said, barely cracking a smile. "How do you feel?"

"Like I picked a fight with a barn and lost."

"Oh, you lost big time, but… you *are* alive, and you're going to pull through, so I think we can call it a win."

Striker was like the rest of us in a lot of ways. He was a huge tank of muscle and testosterone, but he was also the quiet one of the group, the one that stayed on the edge. His long ash brown hair ran down to his shoulders and was almost always tied back. A quiet an assuming knowledge lingered on his sharp features. Most of his thoughts were communicated silently.

I tried to sit up, but all I could feel was pain. "Blood?"

"I'll get you more now. Hold on."

He moved across the room and I took in my surroundings properly for the first time. We were in the medical bay on Xerxes-1, the unit's designated airship. "Are we heading for his HQ?"

"Yep. Heading north west for Minnesota. You've been out for about thirty minutes, and probably another ten before we got to you. We have fifteen minutes until we land."

Striker came back over and connected a fresh bag of blood to my drip. The dark red liquid flowed down the plastic tube and into my body, filling me with a warm and invigorating rush. It gave me the little strength I needed to sit up.

"What can you do to get me combat ready in fifteen minutes?" I said. Striker just laughed at first.

"You broke both arms, both legs and have compound fractures across your body. You had a wooden beam sticking through your hip and lost so much blood you nearly died."

"But here I am."

"Here you are," Striker reiterated.

"My bones are already healed, my hip looks..." I glanced down. It was bandaged, but I knew the skin would have healed over by now. "Better, and I've got a body full of fresh blood, so what's the problem?"

"Look," Striker said as he set his clipboard down. "We both know that our healing abilities are extremely advanced, even beyond that of most vampires."

"Yep."

"But what you've just gone through is the equivalent of intense chemo. I have never seen a guardian take that level of physical punishment and survive. The fact that you're even talking to me right now is a medical marvel."

"Write your case study later," I said. "I'm asking you what I need to be combat ready in..." I glanced at the clock on the wall. "Eleven minutes."

"Can you stand up?" Striker said, posing the question as a basic challenge.

I ripped cords and tubes from my body before standing on my feet, my legs shook slightly underneath me. I was a little dizzy, a little weaker than usual, but I could already feel my strength coming back.

"See? I'm fine. Another ten minutes and I'll be good as new," I said. "But if there's anything you can give me to speed things along..."

"Davian needs to sign off on that," Striker said, looking unsure of himself. "You're pushing yourself too far Hunter. If you carry on like this, you *are* going to die."

"He's got my mate, Strike," I said. "I will get her back or die trying. It's that simple."

"Well hoo-fucking-rah." Davian thundered into the medical bay, a cigar dangling from his lips. "He actually survived."

"Survived and ready to roll out. Ready for evac in ten."

Davian laughed. "You got to be out of your fucking mind, Hunter. You go down there and you're as good as dead. I can't lose you now, even if you are a giant pain in my ass."

I looked the commander square in the eye. "I'm not asking for permission. If you want me to stay on this ship, you'll have to kill me."

Davian sighed. "I'm fucking tempted Hunter, seriously." He looked at Striker. "Are you really clearing him for combat?"

"I would stake my medical license on this man staying in bed," Striker said. "But the patient has demonstrated a remarkable recovery so far. He will need some... chemical assistance to make sure he's combat ready, but that sort of intervention needs clearing by you."

Another loud sigh. "Christ Hunter, you're really asking us to pump you full of drugs?"

"It wasn't a problem when you turned us into guardians," I said, "so what's so different now?"

Davian rolled his eyes and looked at Striker. "What would you recommend?"

"We have got a trunk of *Rage* on board, but—"

"No way," Davian said.

I lifted my head. "Sounds perfect. Let's go."

"Hunter that shit has been banned for a reason!" Davian roared. He looked at Striker. "Why is that even here, wasn't it confiscated?!"

"It was," Striker shrugged, "but the drug is damn effective. I kept hold of some just in case."

Rage was an experimental cocktail of drugs given to guardians going into combat. It turned already elite soldiers into unadulterated killing machines. HQ eventually pulled the plug on the project over concerns of uncertain side effects.

The stuff was extremely powerful, incredibly dangerous and a very bad idea.

"It's exactly what I need," I said. "Give it to me."

Davian blew out plumes of smoke. His attention flickered between me and Striker. "I'm not approving this. You're not putting that shit in him." Davian turned for the door but stopped before leaving. "Can you fucking believe this?"

"Sir?" Striker asked.

"That son of a bitch, Hunter. He had a secret supply of *Rage*, and he pumped himself full of the shit before breaking orders to join a top-secret mission." He looked back at me, his brow furrowed hard. "Can you believe that shit?"

"He's always had an insubordinate streak in him," Striker said.

"That he has," I said. "And he'll bear the brunt of any punishment HQ will throw his way."

Davian nodded before looking at Striker one last time. "Do what-ever you have to fucking do. We drop in eight minutes."

As soon as Davian left Striker walked over to an indiscrimi-nate panel on the med bay wall and opened a secret compart-ment. He pulled out a small black case and brought it over to me.

"How long have you had this stashed?" I said and sat on the bed. He opened the case and pulled out one of the vials before screwing it into a compressed syringe.

"The day HQ banned it. I thought it might give us the upper hand one day." He passed me the syringe. "Shoot it in your leg just before we jump. You'll get about twenty minutes off this."

I stood back up and took the syringe. "I appreciate this. Thanks."

"Just don't get yourself killed. Let's go."

We left the med bay and met the others in the ship's cargo hold. Everyone was getting ready, preparing to drop into Harkin HQ.

"The bastard lives!" Charge said enthusiastically as we walked in. We clasped hands. I did the same with Hammer, Ash and Mac.

"Good to see you're still alive, Hunter," Ash said.

"It's Hunter," Hammer laughed. "It'll take more than a mile-drop to kill him."

A figure materialized on the air in front of me, it was Zero, the stealth-op of the group, the assassin. Though still much bigger than a normal person, Zero was the most slender of the group.

"Death waits until another day, aye Hunter?" he said.

"That it does."

We all suited up, pulling on our body armor and loading our preferred weapons. Charge had a belt full of explosives. Mac had a Kevlar staff with deadly electrical probes. Zero preferred quiet weapons. Silent handguns and knives made up his arsenal. Hammer had his huge fucking war mallet.

Nothing new there.

Ash stuck to medium-sized guns. He liked the default assault rifle that we were all required to carry, but he was also a dab hand when it came to long range sniping. Striker was there to patch us up, but he also had his bow. Many underestimated the weapon, but he was fucking lethal with the thing.

Briggs and Rocky would be staying on the ship. Briggs would keep the bird circling while Rocky provided tactical insights from above. His equipment allowed him to get a bird's eye view of the thermals from above.

Davian normally stayed behind as well to direct the mission with Rocky, but he was currently loading up his twin shotguns. It looked like he was joining us this time.

My own setup changed each time. Tonight, I went all out. I had an assault rifle and a shotgun on my back. Twin pistols holstered on my waist along with several grenades. I had a serrated combat knife tucked into my boot too.

"Sixty seconds!" Davian roared down the cargo hold, his voice carrying over the whirr of the ship's engines. We all lined up at the rear doors, which slowly opened onto the night sky. They dropped down until a downward sloping ramp was the only thing separating us from the heavens.

The room roared with the sound of wind and engines.

I felt a hand on my shoulder. Turning around I saw Striker. He nodded at me and I nodded back. I slammed the rage syringe into my thigh and instantly felt its sinister effects take place. Fury, adrenaline and testosterone ripped through my body as a cocktail of mayhem.

"Go!" Davian screamed from the rear. "Go, go, go!"

One by one we ran to the edge and dropped into the night. I no longer felt the pain or weariness of my near-death experience. My legs pumped down the ramp and I launched into the heavens. Wind rushed over my ears and the distant lights of Harkin HQ glistened on the ground below us.

Eight figures of death plummeted through the sky, sailing towards earth to complete our mission.

It was time to get my mate back.

Or die trying.

15

RACHEL

*T*he room was dark and quiet. Tight ropes bound me to the chair. The psychic vampire witch sat across from me, tied to her own chair. Harkin slowly circled us, his deliberate footsteps echoing around the room.

"The game is very simple," he said. "If you lie to me, then the other one gets hurt." He stopped and held a cattle prod in the air, hovering it between the two of us. Harkin looked at me. "What happens next? Where is the tomb?"

"I don't know," I said, "It told us to—stop!"

Harkin jammed the prod into Saydra's neck, blasting the witch with violent jolts of electricity. She screamed, nearly tipping back in the chair. He stopped after a few seconds.

"Shall we try again?"

This time Harkin looked at Saydra. "I know you can see inside her mind. I know you already see the truth. Tell me what happens next. Where do I take the amulet?"

Saydra looked at me. This was the woman that assigned missions to the guardians based off her visions. She was the reason Hunter had found me in the first place. I fully believed she could see the secrets in my mind.

"I can't see," she said. "Her mind is clouded—no!"

It was my turn to get electrocuted by the cattle prod. Harkin stabbed me in the neck and I screamed as electricity made my entire body seize up. The pain was truly unbearable. I couldn't let this happen to Saydra again.

"Do we all understand the rules now?" the twisted vampire said as he went back to circling the two of us. "You are both torturing each other until you tell me the truth." He laughed to himself. "It's genius when you think about it. Doctor Stone! Would you please tell me what happens next? Where is the tomb?"

"Why are you so sure that I know?"

He held the prod over Saydra's neck again. "No games. Hurry up now."

"Okay!" I said. "Just don't hurt her! I might have an idea where the amulet is leading us."

"Don't tell him!" Saydra screamed.

"It's okay," I said. "I won't let him hurt you anymore."

"Hurry!" Harkin roared.

"Indianapolis," I said quickly.

Hunter paused and drew the prod back. "Indianapolis? But... why were you coming here? Why come to me?"

"We need to activate the amulet three times to make a triangle. One point in New York, the other in Louisiana, the third is here. Then we find the tomb at the triangle's center." Harkin weighed up the information briefly before attacking Saydra again. "Stop! Stop!" I screamed.

"Is she lying?" he said to Saydra.

"No—" she wheezed.

Harkin got me again. This time was worse than the last. He turned and looked at the witch. "We're done playing games. I know you're both lying. Pay attention, Saydra, you can survive much longer than Doctor Stone. You tell me what you know, or I kill her."

"Don't hurt another hair on that girl's head," Saydra warned.

Harkin pressed the prod against my neck. "Last chance. I will kill her. I'm not joking."

I fully believed Harkin, but I'd rather die than give up the amulet's secret. I'd figured out the location right before I had to jump from the plane. The spot opposite to the triangle's center, all the way on the other side of the planet: Ayer's Rock, Australia. A mountain in a dead desert, right at the country's center.

"Your greed will kill you," Saydra warned.

The prod clicked as Harkin prepared to torture me again. "Have it your way—"

"Okay, wait!" Saydra said. "I will tell you the truth. The girl has told you part of it already. The tomb is in Australia. Ayer's rock."

Harkin finally pulled the prod back and smiled. "Now why does that feel like I finally got the truth? Ah… because I can see the defeat in your eyes."

"That's not defeat," Saydra scowled. "It's exhaustion. You already beat all of my power out of me. The last drop I have left, it will take everything I have to use it."

"What are you talking about?" Harkin said.

Saydra's answer came in the form of a raw and primal scream.

A word came from her lips. I couldn't discern what it was, or what it meant. It was an ancient word, maybe from a lost and ancient tongue, but I could feel the power coming off her.

With her primal roar a wave of powerful energy exploded through the room, the witch at the blast's epicenter. The shockwave smashed into Harkin and sent him flying across the room. He crashed into one of the dark brick walls and collapsed to the ground as a motionless figure.

My own chair blasted back with the force and I crashed against the floor, still bound to my seat. I heard Saydra and Harkin groaning, but I couldn't see either of them now. Then a face came into view, it was Saydra. She crouched down and untied me.

"We have to be quick," she said. "There isn't much time."

We both jumped to our feet. I grabbed the amulet off the table, and we ran for the door. Saydra lifted her hand, splayed her fingers and the door blew off its hinges. In the hallway we stepped over two guards that had been knocked out by the door and we started running.

"How do we get out of here?!" I shouted.

"With help."

As she said the words, I heard the sound of explosions and gunfire begin to rattle overhead. "Guardians!" I shouted in excitement.

"The boys never fail to disappoint," the witch said with a slight smile.

An elevator took us up from the basement level. The doors opened into a grand marble lobby, and we found ourselves right in the midst of the battle. The deafening blast of gunfire and explosions rattled our ears. Hunter and his guardians were doing battle against Harkin's magic-fueled goons.

As soon as the doors opened, we found ourselves staring at a pack of Harkin's men. They were firing upon the guardians on the opposite side of the room. The pack turned upon hearing the doors and paused momentarily. Their eyes were all a ghastly shade of electric violet.

"The prisoners!" one yelled. "Get them!"

Saydra immediately slammed the close door button, but Harkin's men were sprinting at us, we had no time at all. I closed my eyes and winced, hoping that anything could protect us.

The answer came as the amulet exploded in my pocket once more.

A huge ball of light burst from the elevator and vaporized the vampires that had broken away from the main group. They turned to dust in the light but had shielded the others from the attack.

"Get them!" a vampire in the remaining group shouted. "Before she does that a second time!"

"Quick!" Saydra shouted. "I've got no power left!"

The amulet was red-hot in my pocket, and something told me it was out of juice too. "It's done!" I shouted. "We're out of luck!"

Four of the goons were seconds away when three huge figures crunched down in front of the open elevator doors.

"Eat shit and die cocksuckers!" Davian roared, unleashing a barrage of gunfire with twin shotguns.

"I don't know about you!" Charge said as he unclipped two grenades and hurled them at the group, "But I'm having a blast!"

The final figure emptied twin pistols into the heads of multiple goons before looking back at me.

"Hunter!" I shouted. I ran from the elevator and practically threw myself into his arms. The guardians had eviscerated the group and saved us.

"I had a funny feeling you girls would give them a run for their money," he said with a smile. "Now stay close!"

Both Davian and Charge grabbed Saydra. We ran back across the lobby, taking cover behind pillars to shelter from waves of gunfire. I saw the other guardians blurring across the large room, locked in mortal combat with the violet-eyed henchmen.

I saw one guardian suddenly surrounded by three of Harkin's men. He spun a staff in his hands and dispatched them all with elegant precision. I knew it must have been Mac, the combat specialist.

Hammer wasn't hard to miss. He was a juggernaut compared to the rest, charging across the room and swinging his Warhammer around like a Viking out of time.

We were heading for glass doors at the lobby's front when a group of Harkin's men appeared in our path. Hunter, Davian and Charge turned to change direction when we saw another group behind us.

We were surrounded.

"Hey!" a voice shouted from a balcony ahead. "Up here fuckers!"

We all looked up and saw Ash. He fired down at the group in front of us and they turned their guns on him. A second later an arrow whizzed down an exploded in the center of the group. My eyes traced its path and saw another guardian with a bow pointing down.

Striker. The lone wolf.

The group in front were gone, but we still had another group behind us.

"Freeze!" they shouted. "Or we shoot!"

"Okay, you got us," Davian said calmly, dropping both his shotguns to the floor.

I wondered why he was giving up so easily when I noticed something moving through the air directly behind the group. The pillars behind the five vampires rippled slightly, like I was looking at a mirage or a heatwave.

Each of the possessed vampires froze one by one and dropped to the floor before bursting into flame.

The mirage revealed itself, materializing before us as another guardian. Blood dripped from a knife in his hands.

"Good old Zero," Davian laughed as he picked up his shotguns. "What would we do without our sly assassin?"

"All right let's get out of here!" Hammer roared. "Prisoners are secured, and the area is clear. Rocky! We need immediate pickup!"

"Not so fast," a voice said, echoing from a balcony right at the back of the room. We all looked around and saw Harkin. He had a gun in one hand and... something else in the other. I couldn't quite make it out. The vampire slowly descended the staircase leading down to the ground floor, limping as he did so.

"You've made a very fine mess of my HQ. Well done. All of my men are dead, even with the magic of my demon stone, they were still fucking useless. Oh well. I guess I'll finish this myself."

"The game's over dickhead," Davian shouted. "You lost. Now drop the weapon before we fill you with lead."

"No," Harkin said calmly. He reached the bottom of the stairs and stepped onto the floor. "The game has just begun. I have the information I need now. All I need is the amulet. You see, I have won. I got exactly what I wanted."

Hunter laughed. "We have everything. You have nothing. What have you won?"

"Well, I have this," he said, holding up a small control in his hand. He pushed a button and an automated voice suddenly echoed through the lobby.

"Self-destruction sequence initiated. T-Minus three minutes."

"You're fucking bluffing," Davian shouted.

"Am I? Why not ask the eyes you have in the sky? The explosives are right underneath us. 2000lb of plastic explosives. Enough to launch us all into space."

"Uh guys..." Rocky said, his voice coming from a speaker on Hunter's armor. "The info checks out. He's not bluffing. That place is loaded with explosives."

"What's the game, Harkin?" Hunter said. "All we have to do is sprint out of here."

"And all I have to do is override the countdown. We can all be dead in the blink of an eye. So, this is what we're going to do. You give me the amulet, and I give you the control to deactivate the explosives. It's a very simple trade."

Harkin walked through the lobby until he was right at the front doors.

"Now you listen here—" Hammer began.

"Ah, ah," Harkin said. "Take another step and I blow this place to smithereens. That goes for all of you."

"Have you thought this through, dickhead?" Davian said. "If you die then no one gets to the tomb."

"Have you thought it through, commander?" Harkin fired back. "If you don't cooperate then the world will definitely end. If you do... then we'll all still be alive, and all of humanity will worship me as a god."

"Apocalypse is certainly more attractive," Davian murmured.

"Make the trade," I said.

All of the guardians looked at me in surprise.

"Rachel?" Hunter said. "You can't be serious."

"Let him have it. We can still escape here and catch up to him. We'll figure it out. This isn't the end."

"Listen to the girl," Harkin said. "She's the only one here with a brain." He held up the control as if to offer it. "Now give me the amulet."

I fished it from my pocket and held it up. "Along the ground, at the same time."

"Of course."

We counted to three and both threw.

The amulet slipped along the marble in its cloth. The control slid along the floor and stopped at my feet. Harkin shoved the amulet into his pocket and stepped back quickly towards the doors. Just holding the thing looked uncomfortable for him. His nose was bleeding, and he looked in pain, but he had it, nonetheless.

"Until next time guardians," he said. "Good luck with that control."

Harkin disappeared and I instantly looked down at the remote. A timer was at the top, counting back from three minutes. We had one-minute left. Underneath was a keypad and several switches.

"What do I do with this?!" I panicked, holding it up so everyone could see.

"Let me get a visual!" I heard Rocky shout over the radio. "Give it to Charge!"

The guardians all gathered around quickly. I passed the remote to Charge, while Rocky tapped into his visual feed.

"What are we dealing with here?" Davian barked.

"A fucking trick," Charge said. "The timer's started moving at double speed."

"Let's just get out of here!" Hammer shouted.

"Not enough time," Charge said. "Listen up, Rocky, this sort of device will send the ignition sequence over a very specific radio frequency. Is there *any* chance you can run a shortwave scan and send out a signal jam?"

"Will that stop the explosion?" Hunter asked.

"It will do one of two things," Charge said. "Kill us all instantly or deactivate the sequence."

"Rocky?" Davian shouted. "Rocky? Answer the man!"

"Little busy trying to find my signal jammer!" Rocky shouted back over the radio. "Briggs! Stop moving my goddamn things!"

"Haste please!" Charge shouted. The timer was on twenty-five seconds and descending rapidly.

"Got it!" Rocky shouted. "Oh fuck!"

"What now?!" Davian roared.

"Where's the power cable?!"

"Rocky!"

12 seconds.

6 seconds.

4.

"Got it! Just got to hit the switch!"

The radios all went dead instantly, and the lights went off. I closed my eyes and waited for the explosion that would kill us all.

16

HUNTER

I kept tight hold of Rachel while waiting for the blast that would surely kill us all. The immediate silence was penetrated by a shrill and deafening whistle. It was radio interference, and it forced us all to pull our earpieces out.

A scrambled voice came over the radio.

It was Rocky.

"G-Good n-ews!" the stuttering signal said. "We stopped the explosi-on!"

Just as he said that speakers in the lobby started playing again. "Self-destruction sequence initiated, T-Minus 3 minutes."

"Rocky?!" Davian barked. "What's going on?!"

Rocky responded again, the signal a little clearer this time. There was no stuttering, but there was heavy static on the signal. "Hey guys, so we have a little complication. The signal jam has stopped the countdown, but the interference has put the system into an infinite loop, it's going to keep counting down from 3 minutes over and over again."

"Let's get out of here then," Hammer said. "We've got plenty of time to leave now."

"Not that easy," Rocky said. "Harkin's plant supplies the gas lines to the city in the valley below. If this place goes up—"

"The whole town goes up," I said in grim realization.

"Bingo," Rocky said. "So, we have to stop the countdown. It looks like the system is controlled by three separate radio relays. I'll need four teams of two to go to each relay and manually reset them every three minutes while I work to break the loop."

"So, I'm down six men," Davian snarled. "Fucking great. Striker, Ash, you take the first relay. Hammer and Zero, you're on the next. Charge and Mac, you're the third team. Saydra, I'll need you to help me."

"What about us?" I said to Davian.

"Last I checked you've got an apocalypse to stop. You and Rachel both need to get out of here."

"We're coming down to land now!" Rocky said.

"Davian turned to us. Hunter, I want you and Rachel on that ship. Briggs are you there?" he said into his earpiece.

"Where else would I be?" Briggs' voice came in response.

"Picking up your award for smart mouth of the year," Davian growled. "Hunter and Doctor Stone will meet you outside now. You're on a one-way flight to Australia."

"Not looking forward to that jetlag!" Briggs quipped.

A moment later Rocky had run into the lobby. "Okay, let's keep this place from exploding!"

As he ran in Rachel and I left. I looked back at my guardian brothers one last time before heading up the ramp leading onto Xerxes-1. The ramp closed behind us and Brigg's voice boomed from the ship's speakers.

"Ready to go?!" he shouted.

"Ready," I answered.

In a minute we were on the bridge. "Welcome aboard this redeye flight to Ayer's Rock, Australia," Briggs joked as we ran in. "How was your stay with Harkin?"

"Three stars out of ten," Rachel said. "The room service sucked."

Briggs laughed. "Strap in guys, we're going to be flying fast."

"Any sign of Harkin?" I asked as Rachel and I belted up.

"I picked him up on my radar. A private jet left here about five minutes ago. It looks like he's going full speed for the other side of the planet too."

"Then this really is a race to the finish line," I said.

"Oh, for sure," Briggs said. He jerked his hand back, lifting the ship into the air quickly. The ship started to shake, the sound of engines filling the cockpit as Briggs charged for an emergency takeoff.

"Our inflight movie is... use your imagination!" he shouted over the din. "And we will be serving... absolutely nothing! Enjoy your flight!"

He thrust his hand forward again and the ship rocketed forward into the night.

The race was on.

17

RACHEL

*T*he stakes were too high for me to fall asleep. I couldn't stop thinking what would happen if Harkin got there and used the amulet before we could stop him.

We probably set some sort of record for crossing the globe, but the journey still took hours. When we finally broke into Australian airspace, we all became more alert as the prospect of losing settled in.

The archaeologist in me was screaming when Briggs brought the ship down to land directly on top of Ayer's rock. We shouldn't land even within a mile of this thing; it was a one-of-a-kind geographical feature and there was no saying what damage we were doing.

But there were bigger things at stake, like the survival of the whole world.

Precaution could be damned for one day.

Hunter threw a pistol my way, and we ran down the ramp with our weapons ready. Both of our hearts sank as we saw Harkin's ship already there.

"He beat us!" I shouted.

"We don't know that yet," Hunter said.

It felt surreal to actually be running on top of Ayer's Rock, but my inner scientist had no time to fangirl. On the flight over here I wondered how we would even find the tomb's entrance, but a glowing circle at the center of the rock formation answered that question.

As Hunter and I got closer we realized the glowing circle was an entrance to a spiral staircase, which descended directly down into the rock. A beam of bright light was shining up from the shaft, pointing into the sky.

Hunter took the stairs first and I followed quickly behind. We were descending for several minutes until the shaft finally ended.

The stairs opened into a huge subterranean chamber. It was like the entire mountain had been hollowed out to accommodate Halo's new hiding place. We were standing on an elevated stone platform that looked out over a great lake.

A long walkway stretched across the lake, leading to another platform about five hundred feet in front of us. There a giant statue of Halo stood, looking over the chamber and her tomb. Most of the chamber was dark, but a huge pillar of golden light surrounded Halo's statue, which was easily the height of an apartment block.

At the foot of the statue there was a throne. A golden figure sat atop the throne and kneeling in front of the figure was another.

Harkin.

Hunter and I ran across the walkway until we reached the final platform. Harkin turned to look at us, but he didn't seem concerned about our arrival. We didn't even fire our guns, something told us both that it was too late.

Harkin didn't look good.

Dark veins pulsed across his pale skin. Blood ran from his eyes and nose. The amulet was now lying on a bronze plate just in front of Harkin. He looked glad to be rid of it.

"Thank you for returning my amulet," the golden woman said calmly from her throne.

Bright and warm light seemed to emanate from every atom of her body. Her voice was a choral choir in the quiet chamber.

Halo.

"Hunter, Doctor Stone," Harkin said as he looked back at us and laughed. "You're about one minute too late."

"State your wish, and I will grant it," the goddess said. Harkin looked back at her and rubbed his hands together.

"Make me a god. I want infinite strength and power. I will be the new lord of earth; the universe will be my dominion. None will stop me; all will worship me."

"Your wish is granted," Halo said. Light flowed from her and entered Harkin's body. He turned to us, his eyes now glowing with brilliant white light. For some reason his eyes didn't reassure me in the same way Halo's did.

It looked unsettling on him.

"There you have it," he said, his voice sounding like many voices were speaking at once. "Game over. Time to reshape the universe in my image. Killing you both is very tempting, but I think I will make you my eternal servants. Yes… that sounds very satisfying."

Harkin lifted a hand in our direction, but suddenly froze in place.

"Before that happens, we must finish our business," Halo said calmly. Harkin's frozen figure was shaking and trembling in place, a statue of infinite power and world-destroying rage.

"What is this?!" Harkin roared. "Release me at once! I am a god!"

"And so am I," Halo said. "And my power is only limited to my capabilities. I cannot create something more powerful than myself, so I have dominion over you. Welcome to the realm of gods Mr. Harkin, there are plenty more gods out there more powerful than you and me."

"We had a deal!" he screamed.

"And we still do, but a prior deal was made, and that must be satisfied first." Halo turned and looked at Hunter. "You have returned."

"I have," he said.

"You remember our arrangement from last time?"

"Yes."

"So," Halo said, looking at me. "What will it be?"

I froze. "What?"

"You have a wish to make, Doctor Stone," Halo said. "So, what will it be?"

I looked between her and Hunter. "I'm a little lost."

Hunter addressed Halo. "Am I allowed to break my silence now?"

Halo nodded. "You are."

"Hunter?" I said to him. "What's going on?"

He looked at me. "When Trey betrayed Laurelai I was left with no choice but to make a wish last time, so I did. But I didn't make a straightforward wish. I took a deal with Halo."

"What deal?" I asked.

"*Should I ever find my mate, I ask for my wish to go to her.* So... here we are, and the wish finally passes onto you. Enjoy it."

"I—"

I didn't know what to say.

Hunter had made that wish all those years ago, hoping that one day he could find his mate just so she could take his wish.

So, *I* could take his wish.

"You idiot!" Harkin roared, dark laughter coming from him. "You could have wished your friend back to life! The one you betrayed!"

Hunter barely acknowledge Harkin. "I don't know if you've ever seen resurrection magic, Harkin. But people are never the same when they come back. Bringing them back wasn't an option."

Halo snapped her fingers and a bright chime sang through the air. "That is enough Mr. Harkin. No more interruptions until we are done."

A cage of golden light surrounded Harkin now. He thrashed about inside it, looking like he was screaming bloody murder, but we couldn't hear a word he was saying. I looked back at Hunter.

"Why *that* wish? You could have had anything. All the power in the world. You could have *wished* to find your mate."

"That wasn't necessary. I always knew I'd find you. It was just a matter of time. And as for the wish... it would have been wasted on someone like me. I knew my mate would one day make it count."

"So there you have it, Doctor Stone," Halo said in her warm and earthly voice. The soft heat radiating from her was so peaceful and comforting, but even in her immortal and eternal power I could detect the sorrow in her golden song. "Your mate made a selfless wish and passed the opportunity onto you. I now ask that you use that gift, before the time runs out. There isn't long left. Only minutes."

"Damn," I whispered to myself. "Not long to think. You got any ideas?" I said to Hunter.

"A few, but I passed this power on for a reason. What are you thinking?"

"Take away Harkin's powers for one. The world would almost certainly be safer without him running around as a god."

Hunter laughed. "You can say that again."

But then I realized what I had to wish for. There was only really one logical answer. Men like Harkin weren't the danger in a game like this. I could wish for a dozen different things that would keep the planet safe this time around, but there was only one thing that could permanently make us all safer.

"I know what I want," I said as I turned to face Halo.

"Yes child?" she asked in expectation.

"I wish for you to be free," I said. "End the cycle. Release humanity from this game. Mortals have no place taking the power of gods. We're all much safer this way."

Halo blinked, her golden white eyes flowing with tears.

"It has been several thousand years since my sister trapped me here. Nine times I have granted a wish. Three times my tomb was never found. In all those iterations none have ever asked for my freedom. Until now."

"That is what I desire," I said confidently.

"And that desire is beautiful and selfless," Halo said. "But I regret to tell you child that I do not have the power to grant that wish."

Just then a column of brilliant white light descended from the top of the cavern.

It hit the ground and a portal appeared before us. Through the doorway I saw the backdrop of the universe. A million stars and galaxies all twinkling through eternity. A figure materialized in the doorway and walked forward.

She was small, with long black hair and brilliantly blue eyes. A floral headband topped her brow. A long white summer dress flowed from her willowy body. Motes of golden light surrounded her. Grass and flowers sprouted up from her footsteps.

The goddess of all creation. The sister that had imprisoned Halo. Gaia.

"But I do have that power," Gaia said in a soft yet powerful voice. She looked at me, her eyes filling my soul with the sage wisdom of a universe. "Congratulations Rachel Stone. You are what we have been waiting for."

"We?" I asked.

Halo and Gaia both looked at one another. "Yes," Gaia said. "You see, Halo was never really a prisoner here, and we never really fell out. Those were... creative little lies that we sewed throughout history."

"I don't... I don't understand. If she wasn't a prisoner, then what was the point of all this?"

"To find one that could ignore the greed of ultimate power and demonstrate complete selflessness. To find a human that was truly worthy of holding the ultimate power."

Halo looked at me. "To find, a successor. One to take over."

"From a god?"

"Even gods need to retire," Halo said with a smile. "So, what do you say?"

I just stood there, unable to think. "I am not a god."

As I said the words Halo's angelic visage faded away. With the golden light no longer flowing from her body she looked like a regular woman. She had curly blonde hair and dull green eyes.

"Once upon a time, neither was I. I was one a girl from a small tribal village here on earth, thousands of years ago. My name was Yara, daughter of Grennet."

"I don't know who that is," I said honestly.

Halo just laughed. "No one does. I was just a regular girl, just like you. But I found the amulet, just like you, with the help of my mate. A vampire named Leonidas."

Just then Hunter faltered. "Wait, *the* Leonidas? The Leonidas that started the Guardians?"

"The very same," Halo said with a genial smile.

"You see," Gaia said, "you can think of most gods as gatekeepers. Souls deemed worthy to look after great power. I realized fairly early on that even the gatekeepers need guardians. That's why I created vampires. Every goddess has a vampire guardian. You, Doctor Stone, are no exception."

Hunter and I just looked at one another, blinking as we tried to process everything.

"I am not a god," I repeated.

"Maybe god is the wrong word," Halo said. "Maybe *angel* might make more sense to you. I am currently Halo, the gatekeeper of the sun, but my powers are nothing like Gaia. *She* is a true god."

Gaia laughed. "Well... in the eyes of some. So, Doctor Stone. What do you say? Do you want the job?"

I didn't know what to do.

"I... I like my life," I said. "I like working at the museum. I like research. I like... being with Hunter. I'm not sure I want to give that all up to hide in a tomb for the rest of eternity."

Gaia and Halo laughed. "Very little has to change about your life," Halo said. "You can go on living as normal. Most of the time you're just a vessel for the power. I only hide in these tombs now because mortal life became a little repetitive after several thousand years."

I looked at Hunter. "What should I do?"

"That's your choice. But I'll tell you this: whatever you end up picking, I'll be here by your side. I'm your guardian, whether you take the job or not."

"What about him?" I said to Halo and Gaia as I looked at Harkin. The new dark god was still frozen in place, his face a contorted picture of eternal fury.

"Ah," Gaia said. "Well I suppose this is your fist assignment. What would you have done with him?"

"Death seems too harsh," I said. "He definitely shouldn't be a god. His mind is too dark. Is there any way to remove his memory of this last week? Can we undo all the damage this journey has done?"

"There's only one way to find out," Gaia said with another smile. "Do you want the power or not?"

I looked at Hunter one last time. Knowing he was there by my side no matter what made this decision a lot easier. "I'll take it," I said.

As I said the words golden light suffused the air and flowed into my body, starting at my fingertips and working up my arms until I felt it fill every atom of my soul.

A blinding white light filled the dark cavern until the only thing I could see was white.

I took Hunter's hand and held it.

Then there was nothing.

EPILOGUE

RACHEL – ONE WEEK EARLIER

The blinding light slowly faded and as I opened my eyes, I realized I was standing back in the atmospheric chamber at the museum.

The *Shén Tiàoma*, the thousand-year casket that we had opened one week ago, was right in front of me, still sealed. I had a chisel and a hammer in my hand. Looking up I saw Juniper, Dr. Turner, Harkin, and Barry.

"Barry!" I gasped. "You're alive!"

Everyone looked over at my overweight colleague, who stared back at me with marked confusion. "Uh... yeah?"

"Are you going to take all damn night?! Give that here!" Harkin roared as he snatched the chisel and hammer from my hands.

I got an overwhelming feeling of Déjà vu as he started hammering around the edge of the sealed crypt. Looking through the glass walls of the atmospheric chamber I saw a familiar figure standing guard at one of the doors leading out of the room.

Hunter was wearing one of the museum's security guard uniforms. He was standing still, with his hands clasped behind his back. He looked back at me and winked.

"There!" Harkin said as he finished chiseling open the seal. He was about to hurl the lid up once again before I stopped him.

"Stop right there!" I said, practically jumping on the tomb's lid. I was determined to protect the artifact this time. This tomb was still a priceless piece of ancient history, and I wasn't going to let him damage it again. "We extract the lid, *carefully*."

"Then hurry up!" Harkin scowled.

We carefully removed the lid using the hoist that Juniper had prepared earlier. As soon as it was up in the air everyone rushed forward to look inside the crypt.

It was empty.

"Talk about a waste of fucking time," Harkin said as he started pulling off his hazmat suit. "I'll be billing the museum for time, and as for you Doctor Stone." Harkin turned and looked at me.

"Yes?"

"Don't ever waste my time like this again. It's too valuable. You hear?"

"Oh, don't worry," I said. "You won't be hearing from us anytime soon."

With that Harkin and his goons stormed out, leaving Juniper, Doctor Turner, Barry and I alone in the atmospheric chamber.

"Well that's rather disappointing," Doctor Turner said. "Are you okay, Rachel?"

"Oh, I'll get over it," I said through a massive grin. "I'm sure we'll find the Halo Amulet one day."

"Come on," Juniper said. "We can have a spot of tea in my office and debrief. Doctor Stone is right. This is just the beginning."

The group made its way out of the room. I was at the back. Hunter peeled away from his station and started walking with me.

"Do I know you?" I said playfully.

"Oh, I'm new here, miss," he joked back. "I'm on the security team. Did you find what you were looking for?"

"Unfortunately, not. It seems my prediction was incorrect."

Hunter looked at me seriously for a moment. "Any idea where the amulet really is?"

I watched the trio ahead of us and then pulled the amulet out from under my blouse. Hunter's eyes opened wide upon seeing it. I slipped it back into hiding.

"Safe and sound," I said with a smile.

"You know if we've gone back a week in time," Hunter said, "that technically means we haven't had sex yet."

"Well we might have to remedy that fact rather quickly," I said. "Is this new security guard asking the research doctor out on a date?"

"*Date* might not be the right word," Hunter said. "I'm proposing we get out of here straight away so I can fuck your brains out. Are you free?"

"I might just have a space in my diary," I said.

———————

We leapt across rooftops and through the night. This time we weren't running from the threat of death, we were running towards our future.

Our journey ended at a different apartment this time.

Mine.

I was the one to open the door, but Hunter ordered me inside and locked us both in, his bright red eyes devouring me with lustful impatience.

"Strip for me," he commanded.

I took my clothes off as fast as I possibly could, pausing as I noticed a faint trace of golden light shining underneath my fingertips. Hunter came up to me and took my hand in his, brushing his fingers over mine.

"Goddess..." I whispered to myself.

"My goddess," he growled. With a flash of movement, he tore clothes from his body until he was standing naked, just like I was. We came together in a clash of passionate fury. He picked me up off the ground. I wrapped my legs around his waist.

We fumbled our way through the dark apartment and moments

later we were crashing against my bed. Hunter's lips breathed fired over my neck as he kissed me.

"We find a place together," he said, his lips breaking away momentarily to utter the words.

"Together?"

"Together," he growled.

I felt the burning tip of his cock spear against my wet pussy. I gasped at his sheer size and raked my nails over his broad back, my own body arching away from the mattress as he thrust deep inside me.

"A palace for my queen. A temple for my goddess. Anything you want. You get it."

"I like the... sound of that," I panted, barely able to keep hold of myself as he started to fuck me hard. His muscular torso tensed and rippled with each powerful thrust. He was hypnotic. He was unbelievable.

He was mine.

My tight little pussy trembled around his rock-solid shaft. He fucked me hard, his hips digging deep as he punished my tender sex.

"You're mine," he said. "Forever. Mate. Always."

Always.

The words melted me.

My thighs trembled as fire burst through my body and shattered through every atom. I tensed, gasped, shook and rasped against him, praising his name and always wanting more.

"I love you," he said.

"I love you too," I said back breathlessly.

We came together, our sweating bodies shaking and tensing against one another. He flipped me over, mounted me from behind and took me all over again, spearing me with thrusts that were primal and fierce.

I quickly lost track of time.

Our weekend quickly spiraled into a never-ending blur of maddening lust. The weekend became a week, which became a month, which... well you get the point.

His love for me never seemed to fade, and neither did his libido.

We ended up getting a place together in the city. I could never have dreamed of owning real estate myself. I liked my apartment, but I had always rented, and always assumed I would. A researcher's salary is not bad, but it's an expensive city.

Guardians paid well though, apparently, and Hunter had been in the job longer than most people had been alive. Not only did he have enough to get us a place in the city, but we had a 'small' cabin in the countryside which we used on weekends.

Sometimes I'd even come and stay over at Guardian HQ just to see the rest of the guys. They were all meatheads, but they were fun to be around.

And my powers?

Some things had changed. I felt much more in tune with the sun. For the first few weeks I wouldn't have said much was different (apart from my fingertips glowing every now and then).

For the most part I was just aware of this new energy inside of me. It was hard to explain. It was like I could sense this phenomenal power but couldn't quite understand how to access it.

Things became a little clearer when I received a message from Gaia, a few weeks after everything had settled down. She had come to me in a dream, explaining that ninety percent of my newfound power was as simple as holding Halo's energy in my soul.

I *was* Halo now. The spirit of the sun was inside me. I was the beacon for the golden aura.

"*One day you may need to draw on that power to help others,*" Gaia explained. "*Hopefully that doesn't come soon. For now. Enjoy your life as you normally do.*"

And so, I did.

Hunter was lying beside me in bed when I woke, just like he always was. He had a huge smile on his face.

"What's so funny?" I asked.

"Oh, I was just thinking… it's sort of ironic."

"What is?"

"A vampire fell in love with the goddess of the sun. What's that all about?"

"I guess that is kind of funny," I said. "I'd never thought about it that way before. I guess I should pass all household chores onto you. If you disagree, I can burn that sweet behind of yours with my magic sun powers."

Hunter laughed, rolled over and pulled me towards him.

"Oh darling. The only behind getting punished here is yours. That sassy little mouth of yours, its gonna bring a lot of discipline your way."

I just smiled and bit my lip.

"Bring it on," I said.

I couldn't wait.

The End

ALSO BY ZARA NOVAK

Vampire Guardians

Broken

Dark Vampires

Punished (Book 1)

Ravaged (Book 2)

Damaged (Book 3)

Tales of Vampires

The Vampire's Slave (Book 1)

The Vampire's Prisoner (Book 2)

The Vampire's Mate (Book 3)

The Vampire's Captive (Book 4)

The Vampire's Servant (Book 5)

The Vampire's Fate (Book 6)

The Vampire Dream (Book 7)

The Vampire's Shadow (Coming Soon)

Standalone books

The Vampire Game

Trapped with the Vampire

Blood Lust

MAILING LIST

Join my mailing list to stay up to date. It's for new releases only, no spam:
http://eepurl.com/b5tmt5

Follow me on Facebook for updates and general chatter:
https://www.facebook.com/TalesOfVampires

Or just drop me an email:
redlotuspublishing@gmail.com